I0589710

A Panther's Pride Saga

Book 1

CLAWED

Tonya Coffey

Saguaro Books, LLC
SB
Arizona

Saguaro Books, LLC
16845 E. Avenue of the Fountains, Ste. 325
Fountain Hills, AZ 85268
www.saguarobooks.com

ISBN: 9798640047554
Library of Congress Cataloging Number
LCCN: 2020937484
Printed in the United States of America
First Edition

Dedication

To all the JROTC Cadets

Other books by the Author:

New World Series, Books 1-5

Prologue

The sun beamed down, causing sweat to bloom along my brow. It wasn't your typical summer day. The humidity wrapped you in a blanket sucking the oxygen from your body. With each step I took, it was harder to take the next.

Ignoring the pain in my side, I pushed harder. When I ran through the woods with the trees looking down on me, the animals watching as I passed, it was the only time I felt like myself. I wasn't an orphan; one of a dozen kids in the system.

I was me, Christa Taylor.

As I ran, I didn't have to worry about anything but the trail in front of me. My eyes focused on the dirt as my feet made contact with the ground. I didn't have to worry about holes or debris in my path. My brain automatically knew where I should step. I glided over the terrain as if I was the breeze.

So I pushed myself, faster. My arms pumped at my sides, as my breath came and went with gusts. The rhythm propelled me forward, closer to the place where I didn't want to be yet it was inevitable.

I had to go.

Slowing my stride at a two-foot wide stream, I glanced up the hill on my right. The trail ended in the dirt parking-lot, delivering me to my future. I hoped it was for the good but I had a feeling it wasn't.

As I rounded the corner, the sun seemed to blast into my eyes. I squinted from the rays, turning my head slightly. The light grew. Slowing my pace, I peeked up at the ball that came closer. *What the*...Closer it soared. My eyes widened at the phenomenon and I back paddled; however, I wasn't fast enough and it slammed into my chest.

The force sent me to the ground on my butt. I quickly grabbed at my shirt expecting to be on fire or scorched. Instead, there were no visible remnants. No burns, scars or tears. My eyes swept the woods. There was nothing to explain what I'd seen. It was as if it were my imagination. Standing, I looked around once more and decided maybe I was going crazy. Besides, if I burst into flames, I wouldn't have to face what awaited me on the hill. Therefore, I took a deep breath and ascended the last few feet.

The sun shone down as if highlighting the one car sitting at the end. As I neared the blue sedan, my stomach ached. I had hoped a gray van with a middle-aged man and woman would be waiting for me. In their place was an older woman named Ms. Ila.

Taking a breath, I eyed the older woman who had a few strands of grey in her hair. She wore the same black skirt from the other six times she broke the news to me. When she talked, I stared at the small purple stain on the hem just above her right knee.

I tried putting on a smile when I approached the car. After all, I knew it was coming. It had been less than six months. Any longer and I would've thought they actually liked me.

"Hello, Ms. Ila," I said, "is it our one on one day?" I could only hope.

She smiled but her sadness showed in the corner of her eyes. "I'm sorry, Christa."

I let out a half sigh as I shrugged. "I understand. I'm too old." I didn't though. Why would you become a foster parent and only take babies? I was fourteen. Younger than most but too old for the families who cared.

"Don't give up on me." She pulled me into a hug. "I will find you a place to call home."

I tried to look understanding as I crawled into the passenger's seat. Glancing at my red backpack on the backseat, I promised myself I wouldn't get my hopes up. Besides, some people didn't deserve a family…

Chapter 1

I stood on the sideline, watching for my teammates to finish the obstacle course. My blood rushed through my veins with excitement as I waited for them to cross the finish line. I wanted to be on the course with them, to be one of five girls chosen to compete but I wasn't fast enough. I loved running. It was something I did every chance I got; however, my time landed me on the bottom. It didn't register to the Drill Sergeants who pulled the top fifteen cadets from ten different schools. I stood out at my high school, but not at Fort Knox for the summer leadership program. Here I was 1 of 100 cadets in OCPs.

When I first moved to the small town in the Appalachian Mountains, I didn't get a choice of what classes I wanted to take in high school. Because it was halfway through the year, I got the classes no one wanted. The Junior Reserved Officers Training Corps (JROTC) was one of those classes. The JROTC wasn't a class I'd normally picked. After all, they wore camouflage. I didn't mind wearing some green but a whole outfit. What kind of a girl do you ask wears cammies? *Well, I do. Now that I've been in the class for a year.* I wouldn't trade it for anything.

Cheers erupted at the end of the course pulling me from my thoughts. Cadets, decked out in cammies ran full speed from the last obstacle to the finish line. One after another, I watched as my team, along with others, came into view.

"Yeah," I screamed, "way to go."

Rob Anderson was the first runner to cross the line. He looked as if he belonged on the course. When he stood next to the Drill Sergeant, he fit right in. He was the leader of our group and the highest ranking officer in our school. When we returned in the fall, he would be our Battalion Commander. It was a pretty amazing spot to be in.

Tony Jenkins was the second runner to cross. He was hot on Rob's heels at the finish line. When he met a group of girls cheering the race on, he had to stop and say hello. He cocked his head to the side and smiled at them. It was who he was, a big flirt. He played the part well, looking as if he stepped off the movie screen with his dark lashes and green eyes.

"Here she comes," Sarah Jean called out, alerting me to the first girl to come running up the hill to the finish line.

I looked at the crowd to see Mandy Sutton, my best friend, finish the course. We screamed and cheered, proud of what she had accomplished. Right behind Mandy, a slew of OCPs followed. Cadets roared as they flooded the field, welcoming their teammates over the finish line.

I stood foolishly watching Rob—a definition of a country boy, Mandy—the prom queen, Tony— the boy next door and Sarah—the sister you always wanted, hug each other. They smiled and laughed giving one another the praise they deserved. I didn't know why I couldn't join them. Why I couldn't tell them how proud I was of each of them. It was as if I would intrude on their celebration. They had been friends since grade school. I was the new kid. I'd only been a part of their group for a year now.

The crowd settled down when Sgt. Matthews, the Drill Sergeant over our school, stepped forward to read out the times. "I will be awarding a medal to the female cadet who, not only, finished the obstacle course first, but she broke the record for female cadets."

The girls who ran the course stepped forward. We screamed out Mandy's name. The Drill Sergeant smiled. "Mandy Sutton." Cheers erupted as Mandy walked up to Sgt. Matthews. She stood at attention, her hands at her sides, as he slipped a red, white and blue ribbon with a gold medal on it over her head.

"Congratulations, Sutton." He shook her hand.

"Thank you, Sir."

When she turned and headed into the crowd, the girls stopped her and the boys tried to get her attention. I envied her. She was everything I wanted to be. She was smart, pretty and athletic and she had a big family. She knew they loved her. Being in JROTC showed me I could have the family I always wanted. When I turned eighteen, I was signing up for the service. I was going to say goodbye to foster parents and bratty kids who liked calling me names. I sighed. Too bad it was three long years away.

Chapter 2

Five days of getting up at 0500 hrs, I was ready to sleep until 1400 hrs. I didn't mind rising before dawn or the exercises we did, it was the lack of sleep and every muscle in my body felt like wet noodles.

Tonight was our last night as military cadets at Fort Knox. The school's instructors decided to award the schools for the week of hard work by taking us to the local PX so we could do something other than watch TV and play pool.

Hurrying to the shower, I tried to beat most of the girls. Instead, I was next to last in line. When it was finally my turn, I rushed through my routine, dried my hair and dressed in a pair of white shorts and a blue tee-shirt. Standing in front of the mirror, I ran a brush through my stringy brown hair, trying to get it to lay the way it should. When it wouldn't cooperate, I sighed loudly giving up on the task.

I walked out into the hall. Mandy came out of the barracks and met me at the top of the stairs. She had a look on her face as if she smelled something really gross. "Are you seriously going to wear that?"

I looked down at my clothes. "What's wrong with it?"

"Nothing. It's you." She sighed and then smiled. "I got an idea. Let me put some makeup on you."

I shook my head. "I don't like to feel all cakey."

She rolled her eyes. "Cakey?"

"Yeah."

"A dull white cake," she said, putting her arm around my shoulders.

"You should be happy, my hair's down." I normally wore it in a messy bun on the top of my head.

"That's true," she said, with a nod.

We headed down the stairs to the parking lot where the schools lined up next to their bus. "When are you going to let me dress you up?" She just wouldn't let it go.

I laughed. Mandy was all about being pretty. It surprised me she fit into JROTC. Most girls, who joined, didn't like getting their hands dirty. She didn't care, she jumped right in.

"How about when I go on a date?"

She perked up. "Really?"

I nodded as we closed in on Sarah. I know it would never come true because boys didn't notice me. Standing out was something I didn't do, especially when Mandy was near.

The Post Exchange (PX) was a large department store with everything you could ever want or need. The front consisted of a food court, clothing took up the right side and other things went on around in a squareish circle. It reminded me of the peddler's mall with the stores combined under one roof and one place to pay in the center.

Mandy, Sarah and I scanned the clothing racks, trying to decide which Army souvenir we would buy. It wasn't long until Rob and Tony joined us. Even though there were twelve kids from our school who came, we were the closest. They welcomed me into their group with no care of where I came from. It was the first time I felt special.

"Are you going to buy a shirt?" Mandy asked Rob. "Or are you strictly Marines?"

Sarah and I knew Mandy had a big crush on Rob. They even flirted from time to time. He had dated a girl named Ashley for years. When she found out he was going to the Marines, she dumped him. That was six months ago.

Rob leaned in next to her. "Don't tell my recruiter but I have a drawer full of Army tees."

They just stared at each other making us uncomfortable, so Tony turned to Sarah, because she was next to him, and I walked on into the clothing racks to browse.

From time to time, I'd glance back at my gang. When I spun around the next time, my face slammed into a guy's shoulder blades. I assumed it was a guy or a block wall. My breath whooshed from my lungs and I staggered backward. Just as I was about to hit the floor, a hand gripped my wrist, stopping me.

I grabbed hold of his wrist, steadying my body and my breathing. I'd never live it down if my friends saw me fall on my butt. My eyes lifted to tell him how sorry I was for running into him but when I took in his face, my mouth went dry and all my thoughts slipped away.

He had these amazing green eyes. "Um…I'm sorry." I finally managed, trying not to notice how defined his chest and arms were. He looked as if he could bench press a bus. "I should've been watching where I was going."

He smiled. "No harm done."

I glanced down at his hand wrapped around my arm. His skin tone was tanned more than mine as if he spent every day in the sun. "I still apologize for it."

"Don't." He kept smiling. "I'm not hurt." His eyes dropped to his hand. "I should probably let you go."

I didn't want him to. It was the most attention I'd ever gotten from a boy.

"If I do, you won't fall, will you?"

I cleared my throat, as I shook my head.

When he let go, he looked around the store. "You with one of the schools?"

Fidgeting, I answered, "Yeah."

He extended his hand out to me. "I'm Dean."

I couldn't believe it. Why was he introducing himself to me? He was older, maybe twenty-one and he was cute with his buzz cut and squared jaw. He was definitely out of my league.

"Chris." I took his hand.

He raised one brow. "Is that short for Christy?"

"No," I said, "Christa."

"Huh."

"I know it's different that's why everyone calls me Chris."

"Chris?" Mandy called across the store.

I glanced over my shoulder at her then smiled at Dean. "I'd better go." I took a few steps away then faced him. "I hope I didn't hurt you."

"Nah."

I smiled lightly. "It was nice to meet you, Dean." I meant it.

"You too."

When I walked back to my friends, I took a million deep breaths to keep my heart rate under control and bit my lip to keep from smiling like a fool. I was so nervous, afraid I would fall on my face.

When I rejoined them, Tony stared at me with narrowed eyes. I turned to the shirts next to the aisle so they wouldn't ask me any questions.

My lack of eye contact seemed to fuel Tony's interest.

"Who was that?" He acted as if he were my brother instead of my friend.

"Dean," I said with no emotion, as I picked up a shirt. "I just ran into him."

Since Dean was the first boy they had seen me talk to, I expected them to bombard me with weird questions and silly comments but they didn't. They stared at me for a moment, waiting for me to elaborate and that made me even more nervous.

"I'm starving," Tony said, "Yons want to get some pizza?"

"Sounds good to me," Sarah added.

Mandy shrugged as she took Rob's offered hand.

I let out a held breath, thankful they let it go, and followed them to the pizza stand.

Besides, I couldn't wait to get a slice of pepperoni. The cheesy goodness would take my mind off the cute boy. *Maybe*, I thought, as I looked over my shoulder where he stood. He was gone. As I turned back around, I wondered where he ran off to in a hurry. My biggest question, would I ever see him again?

Chapter 3

I sat and gulped half my coke before I even tried the pizza. A week of only drinking water was hard especially when you drank pop for breakfast every day. I needed my caffeine boost and I didn't drink coffee. *Yuk.*

The pizza smelled heavenly. The way the cheese dripped off the sides with a golden color made my mouth water. I took a big bite, relaxing into the back of my chair while the tomato and cheese teased my taste buds.

My eyes floated over Tony and Sarah sitting across from me. Walking across the PX was Dean. His eyes were locked on my location, as he strolled down the aisle. I glanced over my shoulder to see if he was eyeing someone behind me instead. When I turned back, he put his hand up and grinned. I almost choked on my pizza.

"Chris," Dean called, as he walked up to the table.

I forced the bite down, hoping I didn't have it all over my face. "Hi." I felt my friend's eyes on me so I quickly turned to them. "Guys this is Dean. Dean, Mandy, Rob, Tony and Sarah," I introduced them going from my right around the table.

He gave everyone a quick nod. "It's nice to meet you." He introduced his two companions. "This is Carter and Becca."

I glanced at Carter. I thought Dean's eyes were intense. Carter's eyes were a blue color that reminded me of the pictures of water around deserted tropical islands. His hair was shaggier than Dean's. The tips of his brown hair were golden like he'd spent one too many days in a chlorine filled pool. He was also tall, taller than most boys, close to six foot four.

"Hi," I mumbled. He didn't say anything. He just stared. My body broke out in an intense heat. My heart hammered against my ribs. I felt as if I couldn't breathe and I was starting to panic.

"When I saw you walk away, I remembered seeing your friends."

I ignored my nerves and refocused on Dean. "You saw them before?"

He nodded. "This morning."

He saw them run the course. I tried not to slouch from the disappointment I felt. It was the only thing we had done today.

"My team and I saw how well you all did on the course. To prove it, we'd like you to come to another camp that'll start in a couple of weeks."

I looked at Rob and Mandy. He watched them run, so he was asking them, not me.

"Chris?"

I turned to Dean. "What?"

"Would you like to be a part of it?"

"Me?" I was surprised. "I didn't run." Why would they want me to come?

He smiled, as he glanced up at Carter. "We are inviting all five of you."

Really? I glanced at each of his friends. *Why?* I couldn't figure out why or who would invite us. It had to be some kind of joke.

Rob asked for me, "What is this camp you're talking about?"

"It's a summer training facility for high school cadets who are interested in special operations. We make the habit of only asking JROTC students to attend because they already have a basic knowledge of the life we live."

I wondered, "Are you affiliated with the Army?"

"We are an elite group," he added vaguely. "This summer is the first that we've started in this state. We have other programs in Missouri and Georgia."

As I listened to him, I remembered some of the other kids talking about a group of SOPs watching the training. They told of a General walking with the group, talking to certain cadets. There were rumors of a secret organization that were looking for their next recruits. *Is it true?*

"Where is it?" I asked.

"Eastern Kentucky," Becca answered, as she slid in next to Tony. "I'd insist you come, handsome." She pressed her cheek against his and let out this sigh that sounded more like a purr. "We could have some real fun."

A little attention was all he needed. "I'm in." He grinned causing the rest of us to roll our eyes. He was ridiculous.

"I don't know," Rob answered.

"Come on, Rob, it's a great program. You'll learn from Captains, Lieutenants and other Sergeants," Dean explained, "We only consider the best and from what I saw. You guys are part of that group."

Even though I wasn't the best, I wanted to do it. I wanted a guarantee that I would be part of their elite group. My chance at the family I'd always wanted was in my grasp. All I had to do was say yes to them right here, right now.

I have to take the chance. "I'm in."

"Good," he said, as he pulled out his phone. "Give me your number and I'll send you the info."

I felt as if I sunk into my seat. "Um, I don't have a cell phone."

His eyes widened. "Seriously?"

Becca laughed. "I thought everyone had a cell phone."

I felt bad for having a foster family who didn't buy me things like the other kids. We got an allowance and I saved it for other things. At least I got clothes and food from them. I wouldn't complain about that.

Rob handed Dean his phone instead.

"I'll see you all in two weeks." Dean smiled then turned and walked away.

Becca gave Tony a peck on the cheek before she followed Dean and Carter. When they got so far, Carter stopped as if he didn't want to but had to. He turned toward us. His eyes locked on me, staring as if I had two heads. *Why did he do that?* Then in a rush, he turned and hurried after his buddies.

Chapter 4

The morning was hot. It was even stuffy as I stood next to the road waiting for Rob and Sarah to pick me up. My house was the third stop on the way out of town. Mandy's was the last. She lived closer to the county line. Her road took us to the highway that led out of the county.

While I waited, I thought about my guardians inside the three-bedroom trailer. I gave them the permission slip I'd downloaded at the library. May, my foster mom, didn't ask any questions. She just filled it out and gave it back to me. I don't think she even read it. If she had been my real mom, would she object to me going?

Sighing, I glanced over my shoulder at the doublewide. It set back away from the gravel road. Two big trees grew in the front yard and the back had a small round pool that was four feet deep. The property wasn't as fancy as the home I lived in when I was ten. That dwelling was a big two-story with a rounded driveway. I even got my own room. Here I shared a bedroom with two younger girls.

It wasn't bad. May and Jerry didn't hit me or lock me in my room like some places that I stayed. However, it would be nice to have them notice when I came home sometimes with scratches and bruises.

As soon as you turned off the side road on to this one, it was two miles. I liked running it in the mornings before school. The peace and quiet were wonderful. It was the only place where I'd lived, I didn't have to worry about traffic.

The roar of an engine came down the road. The black Jeep Cherokee came into view making me smile. I picked up my duffle and said a silent goodbye to the family inside. *It would be nice if you were outside, waving me off.*

Rob pulled into the driveway. With one last look at the house to see if anyone was looking out the window, I climbed into the back.

"Hey, Chris," he said.

I smiled. "Yons excited?"

Sarah sighed. "I guess."

I laughed as Rob backed out and turned back to the main road. Sarah was never excited about anything.

On the way to Black Mountain, where the facility was located, I thought about the three who invited us. I think what made me question all of this was their age. Why was there a special camp for high school kids ran by college kids? We asked our teacher, 1SG Jones, about it. He made a few phone calls and discovered it was a legit place. Their sole purpose was to recruit high school students, who already knew the basics of the military lifestyle so they could skip Basic Training and go into Advanced Individual Training (AIT).

I couldn't help but think about Dean and Carter. Dean was cute. We'd already talked without me falling on my face, so I was confident he wanted to talk to me more. Carter was different. He was cute too but there was something about him that was odd. I couldn't take my eyes off him, as if I were drawn to him, somehow. In a way, it scared me.

Taking a deep breath, I knew realistically neither of them would be interested in me. Besides, I was there to kick butt and take names so they would ask me to be part of their team. After what felt to be days of driving on a gravel road, through a dense forest, we reached a gas station. We were instructed to fill the vehicle's tank, because there would be no other signs of life until we arrived.

Topping the hill, we were welcomed by a billboard that was a four by eight piece of plywood, with a white background and bright red letters that read, *Enter At Your Own Risk.* It was like a jack-in-the-box, popping up at anyone who drove up the road.

My eyes locked on the sign as Rob slowed his speed. The car crawled pass the billboard at ten miles an hour. A lump rose in my throat. My eyes darted around the forest but it was so thick, you couldn't see five feet beyond the border.

A few hundred feet more and we came to a stop. No one said anything. They stared out the windshield as if an elephant stood in our way. I quickly scooted to the side, looking around Rob's seat to see what blocked our path.

My eyes widened at the gate that was as big as a Mack truck. A second sign hung on the gate, *Last Warning*. The lump that was in my throat felt as if I swallowed a softball and it wouldn't go down. I coughed and finally forced it to my stomach. Every horror movie ever made slipped through my mind, in big flashing lights, warning me to not go inside. *Don't open the gate*.

Rob and Mandy opened their doors and climbed out. I wanted to scream at them, to beg them to get back in the vehicle and turn the car around. Who in their right mind walks through a gate with a warning on it like that?

Sarah and Tony climbed out, following Rob and Mandy. I suddenly didn't want to be in the car alone so I followed them to the gate.

I hugged myself, as I walked toward the metal door, looking up at the giant trees hanging over the road. Their limbs were akin to canopies to the drive. Then I focused on the gate. Two crossties anchored the fence on either side of the road and a chain that was as wide as my arm tied the metal gate to the posts.

As we stood there, surrounded by the most secluded woods in Kentucky, I wondered if anyone would notice if I never made it home.

Chapter 5

As we stood at the gate, we wondered if we should climb the fence or wait until someone came to let us in. I voted on waiting. Only an insane person would cross it after reading the warning that was displayed in bright orange writing. However, we didn't wait long. Dean showed up, emerging from the thick forest. He quickly took each of our hands in a greeting.

Dean looked yummy in his PT clothes and I wasn't the only one who was staring. Sarah watched his every move as he unlocked the gate and pushed it open for us.

"Head on up to the cabins. Becca is waiting for you at the one you'll be staying in."

He waited as we climbed into Rob's jeep and drove by. I turned and watched him close the gate behind us and relock it. *There's no way out*, I thought with a sigh.

A dirt road led us to the facility. There were eight average-sized cabins; four on each side of the path. A few were newer but the ones on the left had been there for a while. The lumber was faded gray while the others were a honey color. At the end of the road, a rectangular cabin set with windows all across the front and double doors at the left end.

Out in front of the building, a flagpole stood. The colors hung proudly, displaying the American flag and a smaller black one with the words Army across the top and Pride on the bottom. In the center was a cat. I couldn't make it completely out but I figured it was their mascot.

Rob pulled in front of the first cabin on the right. Becca stood on the porch. She looked like a supermodel standing on the end of a runway, displaying her own PT uniform. Her caramel skin tone looked as if she lived in the sun. She was tall and her hair was wadded up in a ball on the top of her head, in a nest of ringlets.

I stepped out of the car. "Hello, Becca."

She smiled. "Chris. How was the drive?"

Mandy sighed as she got out. "Long."

"Trust me I know." Becca laughed.

Tony emerged from the backseat. He gave her a good look. "Where's your cabin?"

"Maybe I'll show you." Her grin widened.

As I glanced at them, I swear Tony blushed. It was the first time I'd ever seen him act that way.

"This is your cabin. There are six cots inside." She opened the door and we followed her inside. "Showers are on the left, toilets on the right."

"We're staying together?" Sarah sounded surprised.

"It'll be OK," Mandy said. "We'll make a schedule."

My eyes floated around the décor. There were new bunk beds and a big couch with a TV in the back. It wasn't a resort but it was clean.

"Mess hall is at the end of the trail." She put her hands on her hips. "Now get settled and change into your PT clothes. When Dean gets back, he'll start you on warm-ups."

She strolled over next to Tony. "I'll see you tonight at the bomb fire. We decided to have a little get together so everyone could meet." She stood inches from him, her finger tapping his chest lightly.

I tried not to stare but I was intrigued. No girl ever made him look as if he was ready to run but afraid too.

"Can't wait," he managed to say.

She smiled and slipped by him out the door. Tony turned to watch her.

Rob wrapped his arm around his shoulders, both of them watching her saunter away. "She's going to break you."

Tony stared as Becca welcomed a new carload of boys and a girl to the cabin next to us. Then he mumbled, "I might let her."

Chapter 6

Mandy sighed. Her emotion brought me back to the girls at the back of our cabin. She and Sarah walked around, looking at every square inch of the interior.

"Do you think this is kind of creepy?" Mandy asked me. "'Cause I do."

I shrugged. "I like it." It reminded me of when I was eight and lived with this family who lived by the lake. It smelled like fish all the time but it was the one place that felt like home.

"You would, Chris," Mandy added, "You could live in a cave."

Her eyes widened after she had said it. I knew she didn't mean anything by it. It wasn't her fault my foster mom was a mean woman. When I was twelve, she used me to take her frustrations out on. I ran away after the third time. The police found me living in a cave. Mandy was the only person I had the courage to tell.

"I'm sorry," she whispered.

I gave her a half smile. It was OK. She didn't mean anything by it.

"At least there's a party later," Rob called, as he tossed his bag on the bottom bunk. We can unwind." He grabbed hold of Mandy's waist and pulled her against him. He stared down into her eyes for a moment then kissed her lips.

"It'll be fun," I added.

Sarah sat on the bottom bunk. "I'll be alone, as usual."

I frowned. "What are you talking about?"

"Everybody'll be off doing their own thing."

"No," Mandy and I said together. "You won't."

"Mandy will be with Rob and you'll be with Dean."

Dean, I thought. I don't know about that. *Maybe*. "I won't."

"We'll see."

A knock echoed on the wooden door a few minutes after we changed into our exercise clothes. Dean opened the door and walked in. He took in the five of us, running to stand next to our bunks.

"How do you like your home away from home?" Most of us nodded. He continued, "First things first. Come have a seat." He walked over to the couch and waited until we joined him. When we sit, he sat next to Sarah.

It surprised me. He invited me, didn't he? I spoke to him at the PX. It felt like we had some sort of chemistry. *Didn't we?* Why was he sitting next to her, when I had an empty seat next to me?

"Our facility is secret to most people. When the two weeks are over, you can't blabber about it to anyone." He eyes each of us with a warning. "The facility started years ago in Missouri and branched out until we decided to plant some roots in Kentucky."

"What kind of team is this?" Rob asked.

"The facility is known for Recon. We will run mock missions, hostage situations and battle sequences to see if cadets can withstand harsh training situations similar to Special Ops."

"Special Ops?" Rob commented. "Those teams consist of experts with years of combined service. How is it possible to start a team with no training and they be considered as one of these elite units?"

"Great question," Dean answered. "It's simple. We are 'different' than any other Special Ops. You can't put a football team and a basketball team on the tennis court and expect them to play with their rules. Our Recon group specializes in scout missions. We are different. We would never say we were better than the official teams."

"So why focus on high school?" Tony asked.

"Simple," he said with a smile. "You're young."

We all looked to one another with frowns. It didn't make any sense.

I wondered, "Is this an audition for the real team?"

He nodded with a half-smile. "Brains and beauty."

I glared. Was he making fun of me? Mandy eyed me with a questioning look but I ignored it because I didn't know. *Does he or does he not like me?*

"Just because we're here, we don't have to join do we?" Tony asked.

"We don't force our life on anyone. It is and will be your choice."

"We're not all ready to join the service," Sarah added.

"I know. The summer program caters to high school cadets."

Silence filled the cabin as Dean waited for us to ask him more questions. When we didn't, he stood. "Let's get started." He walked to the door. We followed. "We start off each day with warm-ups and a five-mile run. After a week we'll take it to the next level."

I frowned. "I thought this was more advanced than what basic training was?"

"We'll get to it. Since this is the beginning of the Kentucky team, we're going to do things a little different. When we have more people, we'll start the actual training."

"Uh…" Sarah said, "I'm out cause I can't run five miles."

He turned slightly as he looked at her. "You will be running ten, with ease, by the end of the week."

I pulled Sarah out the door. Dean stood on the porch while we lined up in the dirt, in front of him.

"Fall in," he called out in a deep demanding voice.

We hurried into formation, waiting at attention with our hands at our sides and heels together until he called out the next command.

"Right face. Forward, march."

I didn't know why but as soon as the cadence sunk into my ears, I felt like I was home. As I marched to the end of the dirt road, I wondered if it wasn't the forest making me feel at ease.

Chapter 7

When Dean said a five-mile run, you automatically imagined running on a dirt track around a circle about eight times. Being in the middle of the woods should've told me otherwise. We ran on a path that was no bigger than a deer trail that weaved through the forest.

It took us across creeks, over gaps in the ridgeline. I didn't mind the scenery. I was at home in the forest. The smell of new leaves, warm dirt and flowers made me smile. Ever since I could remember, I loved nature.

When I lived in the cabin by the lake, my foster mom called me Snow White more than once. She had joked to my foster dad that the animals flocked to me. I remember when they took me away. There was a deer outside the cabin that watched me leave. It was like I could hear him tell me goodbye.

I pushed the memory away and focused on the trail. It was hard to enjoy my scenery when Sarah wasn't as excited. I did what I said and helped her as much as I could. Tony even stayed back, helping me when Sarah couldn't climb a rock. Rob and Mandy eased through with no problems. I even heard them laughing a few times as they ran alongside one another.

Dean was a gray streak on the course. He flew over the terrain as if he floated, making me wish I was as light on my feet today. When he crossed a hard spot, he would wait until everyone crossed then he was gone again.

At the end of the trail, Dean and Becca were waiting on us. Rob and Mandy stood over to the side. Sarah collapsed on the ground, struggling to pull in a breath. I tried to get her to stand and raise her hands over her head but she was tuckered out.

Dean clapped. "Good job, guys." He walked over and offered Sarah his hand. She took it letting him pull her off the ground. "I thought you couldn't run five miles."

"I couldn't," she said between breaths.

He laughed. "Let's get you some water."

We followed Dean to the mess hall. He pushed the doors open, revealing the best aromas known to man. My mouth watered from the scent of pizza, salty French fries and grilled hamburgers. My eyes widened at the buffet stretched across the wall. If you were meticulous about what you ate, you wouldn't be here. They had food for anyone.

The tables were mostly round with four chairs. Along the windows, rectangle tables had six and eight seats. The interior walls were white but the way the sun shined through the big windows, they looked buttery.

Becca handed us a plate as we got to the end of the line. "Help yourself but don't overdo it." She smiled. "Don't want you puking on me."

As I walked down the line, I couldn't decide what to get. There was so much to choose from so I grabbed a cheeseburger and fries. When I neared the end, I stopped in my tracks. They had slices of chocolate cake sitting out on individual plates. I chewed on my bottom lip then grabbed one. I deserved it. I just ran five miles.

I followed the others to the big table and sat across from Dean. I wanted to ask him about the facility but wasn't sure if he would answer me, truthfully.

"Can you tell me some more about this place?"

"It's a training facility." He took a bite of his hamburger, giving me a satisfied look.

Taking a breath, I asked, "Who owns it?"

"Are you getting interrogated, Dean?" Carter came from behind me and sat next to Dean. His eyes were bluer than the day I saw him at the PX.

There was something about him. It wasn't I wanted to jump into his arms. It was as if he knew me. We knew each other somehow. *Does it make sense that you could meet someone and automatically be connected?*

"I'm only curious." My heart felt like it would beat out of my chest.

Carter's eyes scanned my face. I couldn't breathe while he stared at me. Then he smiled lightly, "It's called Army Pride."

Yeah, I said to myself. *The flag hanging on the flagpole.*

"So who runs it?" Tony asked.

Carter grinned. "My grandpa does." He scooped a spoonful of chocolate ice-cream into his mouth. "This is the third facility in fifty years."

Where did he get that? I wondered.

I watched him eat the ice-cream that I secretly wanted because chocolate was my favorite. "Then you have a lot of members?" I forced my eyes away from the chocolaty goodness to his face.

"We do," he answered," Over a hundred."

I figured there were more. Did they not need hundreds at each facility?

Rob asked, "Is everyone in the Army?"

"No," Dean answered, "One facility is Marines and the other is Air Force."

My mind raced as I ate. I wondered what their specialty aloud girls. If they had a lot of girls on their team? Why would we be here doing this if we wouldn't be allowed to participate?

After we ate, we walked out into the midday sun. I followed Dean and Carter, watching them as they headed to the cabins on the other side of the drive.

Dean turned to us. "You get an hour break then meet me in the field behind your cabin." He gave a quick wave and climbed the steps to the cabin across from ours.

"What exactly are we doing behind the cabins?" I called out.

Carter turned to face me. A smile played on his lips as he said, "Self-defense."

Tony joked, "Karate?" He did a strange bird move that made everyone laugh.

Carter smiled at me causing my stomach to do a little dance. "Something like that." He winked and I swear my knees felt as if I would fall on my face.

Wow, I thought, *What was that*?

I couldn't believe the cutest boy I'd ever seen in my life winked at me. I had an eternal smile that could melt Antarctica. Then I fused at myself. I wasn't here to meet a boy. I was here to prove I belonged. I wouldn't let a cute boy stand in my way of my dreams.

As I caught up with Sarah, she moaned at the bottom of the steps. "I want to lie down."

I took hold of her arm. "Come on." I helped her up the steps and to the cot. When she was comfy in her bed, I laid on my own. I closed my eyes and replayed Carter winking at me in my mind. Even though I wasn't letting him ruin this chance for me, it was still the best minute of my life.

Chapter 8

The field behind the cabin was split into two sections of mats. Becca stood next to one and Dean next to the other. They didn't have to give us the order; we automatically knew to split up: girls with Becca and boys with Dean.

Mandy, Sarah and I stood on the edge of the mat while Becca explained the rules of grappling. I'd never been in a fight before so I wasn't sure how to hold myself. It was nice getting a rundown of what I should do if I happened to get into a brawl one day.

Mandy volunteered to go first. I knew Mandy was a natural at everything she did. It proved it when she squared up with Becca; two girls tall like models, hair in the perfect ponytail. It was as if Barbie was ready to fight Malibu Barbie.

Mandy readied her stance. Her fists were up next to her face. Becca gave Mandy a little smile and swung. I sucked in a breath as Becca's punch grazed Mandy's cheek. She dodged it just in time. Even before I knew what was happening. It went on and on with Becca and Mandy trading blows, dodging strikes and throwing haymakers. Sarah and I stood flabbergasted, watching them.

After studying them for a few minutes, I didn't want to get into a ring with Becca. I was terrified. Nevertheless, it was my turn. I had to put on a brave face for Dean and Becca or I wouldn't make it to the end. So, I took a big breath and walked onto the mat to face what was to come.

When our training was over, we dragged ourselves through the dinner line. I wanted lasagna but I was terrified it wouldn't settle right from the hundreds of punches I received to the gut. Instead, I picked up yogurt and watermelon, hoping I could keep it down.

I was glad to see the girls weren't the only ones who got their butts handed to them. Tony and Rob both looked as if they had participated in a street brawl. Rob wore his cuts with pride but Tony walked as if Dean broke one of his bones.

Easing into my seat, I sighed. "I hope I can get out of bed in the morning."

Tony sat next to me, carefully maneuvering his right leg beneath the table. "I hope I can walk to the party."

"Seriously?" Mandy wondered, "How about walking in general?"

He shrugged making Rob laugh.

"Well, I don't want to go," Sarah said, staring at her salad.

"Why not?" I asked.

She sighed. "I'm not as physical as you all. I'm beat."

I smiled as I slouched. "And I'm not? I've never worked so hard in my life." When she looked up at me, I saw all her fears. I saw them each time I looked in a mirror. So I couldn't let her feel as if she was alone. I wouldn't. "I'll stay with you that way we can both get some well-needed rest."

"I don't want you to do that."

"Did I just overhear you say you weren't coming to the party?"

I looked up and Sarah glanced over her shoulder at a new face. He was average height but taller than Sarah. His hair was shaggy, nothing like the buzz cuts of most of the boys around the facility. He even had wild colored eyes that were green with a ring of gold around the center.

"It would be a shame for a pretty girl like you not to come to the dance." He hunkered down to make eye contact with Sarah, which caused her to blush. "I'm Ethan by the way."

Her eyes fell back to her plate as she said, "Sarah."

He smiled at her, ignoring the rest of us who stared at him. "I'm expecting to see you there. I want the first dance." He stood up and walked out the door without waiting for a reply.

"Ooo…" Tony sang.

Sarah picked at her food. "He was only being nice."

"Who cares?" Mandy said, "He's cute."

Rob pouted. "Hey."

She patted his arm. "But not as cute as you."

"So what do you say, Sarah?" I asked, "Ethan wants to dance."

I smiled as the entire table started chanting, "party, party."

Sarah's face reddened to the color of a tomato. "Fine. I'll go."

"Yeah," Mandy and I called together.

As we ate, I kept glancing around at the other cadets. Counting Becca, there were six girls. One sat with a group of boys at the table next to ours. She was short but she looked like she had no problem getting up a six-foot wall by herself. She had arms like the boys. The other girl was tall as me with shoulder-length dirty-blonde hair. She sat by herself. It was like she was the only one here.

I thought it was weird there were only six when there were fourteen boys, not counting the ones who seemed to run the camp. I would have to ask one of them about it. Making a mental note that I would talk to Dean or Carter, I continued to eat my yogurt.

Becca joined us before we finished. "Sorry 'bout the beating girls." She had a smile on her face that told she enjoyed each punch. "I brought you a gift." She set a small round jar down on the table. "Use it on the sore spots and in the morning you'll be good as new."

"Thanks," we mumbled.

She wrapped one arm around Tony as she hunkered down next to him. "Make sure you rub it in good on that leg. I like dancing." She smiled, did an about face and hurried to the main door. When she reached it she yelled out to everyone in the mess hall. "Party starts at 2100 in the training field."

Tony sat there as if he was thinking intently about something.

"What's a matter, Tony?" I teased, "She too motivated?"

His eyes widened as he looked at me. "She scares me."

Rob about choked on his soup.

"You're afraid of a girl?" Mandy wondered with a hint of humor on her face.

He narrowed his eyes at them. "She's not like other girls. She's tough, aggressive even." He groaned. "I like to have the upper hand."

Rob and Mandy tried to hide their amusement at what was not Tony's normal behavior. He liked the attention girls gave him so it was strange when it caught him off guard.

"Don't make fun of me," he said, "I got a bad feeling she's into the whole whips and chains thing." He became serious. "I'm not into leather."

I chewed on my lip to keep from bursting out laughing and put my hand on his arm. I wanted to have his back, to show him I was there for support. "You might like it if you try it." I couldn't help myself.

His faced me with a look as if he could bury me in the woods, where no one would find me, alive. "Thanks, Chris."

I smiled, leaning against him. "You're welcome."

He let out a sigh and shoved a French fry into my yogurt. The joke was on him because I ate it.

Chapter 9

After we ate, we meet Becca outside the mess hall. We got into formation—arms length apart with our arms at our side and faces forward. She then marched us around the side of the building to back. We followed her through the only door at the end. The room was big, probably because it was white. Two windows were at the back letting in a few rays of afternoon sun. Half a dozen rectangular tables and a few chairs filled the interior.

Dean stood at the table in the center. "Gather around."

We each took a position around the table to see what he had planned for our first day of class. Becca joined Dean as he unrolled a map.

"Welcome to Orienteering Training." He smiled. "It doesn't matter where you are in the world, this class will help you."

"We did land Nav in school," Rob said.

"Yeah, did pretty good at a few competitions," Tony added.

"That's good," Dean began, "but did you ever get dropped off in the middle of the woods, alone, with a map, compass and a protractor with more than one point to find?"

"No," Rob answered. "We always had an instructor."

Becca laughed lightly. "This is not your high school land Nav class. It will be hard."

"Land Navigation is essential for our specialty," Dean's voice was serious. More stern than I had seen him the entire time I'd known him.

"It's life or death in some situations," Becca added.

I listened to Dean and Becca talk about what they expected of us. Being hands on was exactly why I loved this camp. They didn't treat us like kids. We were put in a position to fail or advance. You were treated with gloves and told to try again. If you failed, you were sent home.

"This is a map of our camp." Dean pointed at the black squares in the middle of the woods.

If you had looked at a map you would know there are five major colors. Water is represented by blue, vegetation is green, the contour lines are brown and major roads are red but there weren't any roads on this map. It was hundreds of miles of nothing but green.

The brown lines were circles and other lines. They outlined the terrain.

"Do you know the fist method for identifying terrain features?" Becca asked.

That's easy.

We stuck out fists out and smiled. It was the first thing we learned in our class in JROTC. When you hold your fist out your knuckles are Hills, between each hill is a Saddle. All these together are a Ridge with Cliffs on the side. Spurs are your fingers and the Draws are the cracks between each finger. When you open your hand, palm up, a Valley is your fingers and a Depression is your palm.

"As you can see our camp sits in a valley and we're surrounded by ridges. On the western part of the property, there are vertical cliffs, saddles and hills that workaround to the east to where spurs turn into the valley."

Huh? I was confused. How did he see all of that on the map?

As I stared at the map, I could easily make out the waterfall and the path that it took to get to the property. Above it was a saddle that looked like the space between two eyes. On the backside of that, the land became steep with lines touching at times. That was as far as I got identifying the terrain.

"You will study this map because at the end of the week, you as a group will be blindfolded and transported to a remote section of the camp and you will get five hours to get back."

Sarah and I sighed louder than I wanted to. The others looked at us but I pretended as if I didn't see them. This was going to be hard. It was true I loved the woods and was comfortable in it but I couldn't read a map to save my life. I hoped they didn't put me in charge.

"At each checkpoint, your rolls will change. You will each have to perform as the Spotter, the Tracer and the Walker."

Great, I thought.

As Dean took out another map, I hoped I wouldn't get lost because something was out there. I just didn't know what.

Chapter 10

Our bathroom schedule was easy to figure out. It took the girls longer to shower and primp—well Mandy—then the boys so we went first. To my surprise, Sarah had most of the same routines as Mandy which made me feel even more like a Tomboy. Just because I didn't spend hours in front of a mirror, did I not look like a girl?

I did my best to match their styles but all I could muster was a pair of shorts and red v-neck shirt. I didn't have anything that sparkled or was fitted, to highlight my jugs that looked bigger than they already were. I looked like road kill compared to Mandy in her fitted jeans and lacy top and Sarah in her skirt with a ruffled shirt that hung off one shoulder.

Not feeling my best, I gave into Mandy's rant about making me pretty. She pulled out her makeup and went to town. I kept rolling my eyes. She would smack me because I was messing up her ability to apply eyeliner. When she was finished, I stared at myself in the mirror. I couldn't believe my eyes. My brown eyes popped with what she did. Seeing it, actually gave me a boost of confidence something I needed.

The thump of the bass pulsated against the cabin walls, alerting us to the starting party. We headed out the door and around the corner to where the training field was. The mats, dummies and equipment had been removed. In its place was a bonfire. Large logs were situated around the flames for anyone to sit on. A long rectangular table set at the edge of the field with plenty of snacks and drinks to choose from. At the end, a keg stood with Dean and a bunch of boys, who worked at the facility, around it with plastic red cups.

We stood there, looking around at the boys, waiting. I fidgeted, wondering if I should go talk to Dean. I didn't want to leave Sarah because I told her I wouldn't. Besides, if he wanted to talk to me, he knew where I was.

When Becca saw us from the dance floor, she ran up to Tony and took hold of him. She didn't say a word, only smiled and dragged him onto the makeshift dance party zone.

Poor Tony, I thought.

"We're going to get something to drink," Mandy said as Rob pulled her close. "Will yons be OK?"

I nodded as I glanced at Sarah. "Yeah, go have fun."

They walked over to the table, snatching a red cup. I snarled my nose. *Yuk. Why did people drink beer?* It was nasty.

As Sarah and I moved closer to the flames, which wasn't needed since it was eighty at 9:00 pm, her eyes darted to every boy in the area. I knew what she was doing. She was searching for the one who wanted her there. I knew how she felt. I kept glancing at Dean but I had a feeling he didn't really care if I was here or not.

"You came," Ethan said from behind us. We turned to face him. "That makes me believe you might've wanted to dance with me."

Sarah stared at her feet so I answered for her. "She's looking forward to it."

His eyes seemed to shine as he looked at her. I wanted a boy to look at me like that. I slouched.

"What do you say, Sarah." He held his hand out to her. "Would you like to dance?"

Her blue eyes lifted and she smiled. "Sure." Then she took his hand, allowing him to lead her to the dance floor.

I smiled as I watched them slowly get into the rhythm of the music. Well, I watched them fumble around until they finally found the beat. It didn't take her long until her curly hair bounced around her shoulders. I was happy Sarah was having a good time. I glanced at Tony and then to Rob and

Mandy. Everyone was fitting in, but as usual, I was alone. The third wheel in our party of five.

Sighing at my own self, I walked over and sat on a log watching Sarah and Ethan. If Dean wanted to talk to me, he could come over and do it. I wasn't making the first move. I had to have some sort of standards and I wasn't throwing myself at any boy.

"Hi there," a voice said next to me.

I looked up to find four boys staring down at me. "Hi," I tried not to sound as disappointed as I was because it wasn't anyone I wanted to talk to.

"You look lonely. Mind if we join you?" One boy in the back sniggered.

I stood, pointing to the logs far away from me. "There are plenty of seats over there."

He stepped forward. "Maybe we want to sit next to you."

My heart pounded in my chest. The hair on my arms rose. He gave me the heebie-jeebies.

Closer to me, he stepped. His gray eyes narrowed. "Pretty thing—"

"Is there a problem here?" Carter came from behind me, stepping between me and the boy that gave me the creeps. My breath came out fast as if I'd held my breath. I was so happy he showed up. The boys were giving off a vibe that reminded me of a house I was placed in a long time ago. It wasn't a good place.

The boy stepped back, giving Carter room. "We were only talking."

Carter stood tall with an authority over him. "Do you remember out talk, Greg?"

I glanced around to see if Dean or anyone was going to come and help Carter. There were four of them. The boys from the facility stood around as if nothing was happening. My friends were the only ones who held faces of concern. Rob and Mandy even moved closer to the action.

I looked at Greg. The fire outlined the anger in his eyes. "Yes."

"And?"

My eyes darted from Greg to Carter and back again. I wished I knew what was going on because there was clearly something other than what I could see. What had they talked about? *Who were these boys?*

Greg narrowed his eyes as the boys behind him began to look uncomfortable. "I apologize," he growled.

Carter stood there for a moment then smiled. "OK." He nodded. "Go enjoy the party."

Greg's buddies turned and walked away, leaving him eyeing Carter. There was a tension that swamped us. I wished I knew why. Then Greg took two steps back and followed his buddies into the darkened woods.

I chewed on my lip as I stood behind Carter. I didn't know why I felt as if the boys wanted more than to sit next to me. They were odd and Carter came to my rescue. I was so relieved.

He turned to me. "Sorry about them."

The way Carter looked when he said it made me think he actually cared. It was like it upset him for Greg to be near me. I wondered why.

Carter sat on the log where I'd sat earlier. I looked at my seat next to him, wondering if I should sit there or move to a different spot. Truthfully, I didn't want to be alone with Greg out there. Besides, it felt kind of good to be safe. *To heck with it.* I sat down next to Carter.

"Your friends are having fun." He watched them on the dance floor the way I was.

I nodded not trusting my voice.

"Becca likes Tony." He smiled. It was a great one. It made my tummy feel like it was full of insects.

"I think he's intimidated by her."

He glanced at me with that smile. The fire danced across his skin, giving it a warm glow. His eyes were the beautiful blue even in the dark. I quickly rubbed my palms across my shorts, removing the sweat. He made me nervous. *Why?*

"How was your first day?"

"Umm…different." I didn't know how to tell him what I thought of the camp "And secret." I had so many questions.

"If everyone knew about us, our gate would be busting down."

"That gate," I teased. "Have you seen it because I don't think a tank could knock it down?"

He smiled at my attempt at a joke and I felt even stupider. Why couldn't I be like Mandy? She had no trouble talking to boys. As I sat there watching my friends have a good time, I felt as if I was crashing and burning. There was no way I would make it through the night.

Chapter 11

As I sat beneath the stars, a fire burning in front of me and the sounds of music blaring through the night, I tried hard to not seem weird. It was hard since, from time to time, a soft breeze drifted across the field and I got a nose full of Carter. He smelled like a fresh spring waterfall. I couldn't explain it any better. It was just good.

When Carter first stared at me across the PX, I felt strange but as I sat next to him now, I felt something more. It reminded me of the excitement one would feel when you got a surprise or the way your stomach twists when you're on a rollercoaster. I liked how he made me feel. It was so different then what I was used to.

Carter sat quietly watching everyone and I tried to think of something to say or ask. "What's your specialty?" I immediately regretted my question. Why was it when I was nervous the most idiotic things slipped out of my mouth?

He rested his elbows on his knees, thinking of the answer. "Tell me I'm wrong but I get the vibe you'd be interested in the military."

I nodded; surprised he could read me so well.

"We are known for Recon." He leaned in next to me. The scent of outdoor; acorns, dirt and trees filled my nose. "We get sent in before the main team goes in to do the big job." His breath tickled my ear, sending chills down my spine. I closed my eyes and let it wash over me.

Breathing in the most delicious scent in the world, I opened my eyes and asked, "Who runs this facility?"

He thought for a moment then pointed to Dean.

"Then Becca and you?"

He nodded. "I saw on your permission slip you're fifteen."

I rolled my eyes. "It's only a number." I hoped my age didn't push him away. There was a connection between us, a pull I didn't want to be taken away from me. If I knew what home felt like, I'd say it was him.

He smiled. "I would've guessed you were older."

I groaned eternally. "I get that a lot." Being forced to take care of yourself tends to do that to someone. I stared at the fire, wishing I'd listened to Sarah and stayed at the cabin. At least then I wouldn't have been rejected because of my age.

"Your friends call you Chris. What is it short for?"

"Christa."

"I don't think I've ever heard it before." He had a strange look on his face that said he liked it. "It's unusual."

"I know it's odd."

"It's beautiful." He smiled, staring into my eyes. "It suits you."

I glanced at him with my heart racing. My face burned with the embarrassment of his words. No one had ever told me I was pretty. I didn't know if I should tell him thank you. I wanted to but my mouth was so dry it wouldn't work.

He sensed my awkwardness. He rubbed his palms on his knees, cleared his throat as he stood and asked, "Want to dance?"

I tried not to smile too big as I nodded. He reached for my hand and I took it. His palm was rough along the pads as if he constantly used his hands. I had never held a boys hand that felt that way. As he gripped my fingers, I decided I liked it. He led me to the grass where everyone bounced around to the music. Sarah was laughing. Tony smiled when he saw me with Carter. I returned the gesture and focused on Carter.

We danced for a minute then the music changed to a slow tune. I stood there, trying to figure out what to do. Should I put my arms around his neck or just hold his hands. Instead, he stepped into me; his hands went to my waist. I swallowed the lump that tried to rise. He was so close that when he breathed, his breath tickled my cheek.

"I won't bite," he whispered.

I let him hold me against him, moving with his movements. I'd never slow danced before so I wasn't sure how to move. As he held me though, I relaxed into his body. It was a really nice place to be. His aroma blanketed me as the music carried us.

He set his chin on my head. His heart thumped under my ear in a hypnotizing beat. I could get used to the feeling that swarmed in my chest. It wasn't a heaviness that made you scared. It was a warmth that made you comfortable, homey.

My eyes popped open with the realization. Dread rushed through me. I was in trouble. Not the trouble you couldn't escape. It was boy trouble. My pulse raced. I couldn't breathe. My knees wanted to give out. The cutest boy I'd ever met showed some attention in me and I was falling for him. I was doing the one thing you should never do. The worst part, I'd probably never see him again after this camp was over.

Chapter 12

I decided to let myself enjoy the moment, giving into him and the slow cadence as we moved from side to side. Closing my eyes, I let my head fall to his chest. It was strange that I fit perfectly against him to where his chin set on the top of my head. I was taller than the average girl so that made him really tall.

After a few moments, I opened my eyes. I hadn't noticed the music had changed back to a fast pace, making everyone else jump around while we barely moved in the center of them all.

I panicked and stepped back from him. "Sorry."

He frowned, still holding my hands. "What for?"

My eyes darted around to the others dancing. "I didn't know the music had changed."

He smiled. "Neither did I." He twirled me.

It was nice knowing we were both lost in our own little worlds. I took it as a good sign and started dancing along with the others.

"Where are you stationed?"

"Technically, here. It's our job to set the camp up."

"Whose job?"

"Mine and Dean's basically."

I frowned. "You're in charge?"

"Dean runs the camp, all things that relate to the military. I do the rest."

I wondered what else there was. "OK, but aren't you kind of young to be in charge?"

"Eighteen is only a number." He smiled and it nearly took my breath away. "It's more of a blood right," he added.

I was completely confused. *A blood right?*

When the song ended, he took my hand, interlacing our fingers and pulled me off the dance floor. "Dad runs one camp and my brother runs the other. That's why I get to run this one."

He led me to the snack table. "This is a family business?"

"You could say that." He picked up a red cup. "Drink?"

I snarled my nose. "Pop?" He picked up a Pepsi and handed it to me. "Thanks."

As he drank his drink and I picked at the potato chips, I wondered about the camp. How did they get to run an exclusive facility that was part of the Army? It didn't make any sense to me.

"I don't get it," I admitted. "How can you be with the Army but not be."

He sighed. "I really can't tell you any more than that. That's the whole point of the 'audition' to see if you could handle the rest."

I didn't like how vague he was but I was intrigued. Narrowing my eyes at him, I asked, "Are we in danger?"

He thought my question was a joke. "No."

I wanted to know the secret so bad. What could it be? Thinking of being accepted and being part of a tight-knit group, a family. It would be so amazing. It would be the family I'd dreamed of my entire life.

Carter and I headed back to the fire. The crowd started to thin out leaving only a few people standing around. Ethan and Sarah sat on one of the logs. We sat down across from them.

Carter told me about his family. He had a big one and I was envious of him. When he asked me about mine, I didn't tell him anything just that I lived on a small farm. It wasn't a lie. I just didn't tell him it was five acres of field, no animals and no real home with a mom and dad who welcomed me home from school each day.

Above us, the navy sky held tiny twinkling stars and the moon hung at last quarter over the treetops. It was a beautiful clear night. The fire crackled as sparks floated up, dancing around with the heat. Crickets called out from the forest. A whippoorwill even made himself known.

"Do you want to go for a walk?" Carter asked.

I glanced at Sarah who was talking to Ethan. "I don't know." I didn't want to leave her alone with him. It was hard to trust people.

He looked at Ethan and Sarah. "She's in good hands." He stood, holding his hand out for me to take. "I promise."

I stared at his hand as every emotion I ever had slipped through my mind. "What about me?" I looked at him. "Will I be safe?"

He held my gaze for a moment. "I swear."

Coming to this camp was all about taking chances. I took his hand and let him pull me from sitting. "Walking blind into the dark takes trust. Can I trust you?"

He faced me. His face set in a serious expression. "Yes. You can always trust me, Christa."

My name rolled off his tongue as if I was a goddess to him. My heart fluttered and all I wanted to do was wrap my arms around him and let him take me away from my crazy life. I didn't care where it was just as long as it was with him. "OK."

We walked along a worn-out path into the woods. The glow of the orange flames slowly shrunk behind us. After a moment, the only remnants of its existence were the burnt wood smell that drifted through the night. When the darkness became overwhelming, Carter pulled out a small flashlight from his pocket.

He came prepared, I noted.

The crickets called out around us, making the lack of conversation apparent so I tried to fill the void. "Why is Becca the only girl?"

A small grin spread across his face in my peripheral vision. "She came to help search for possible female members."

"Are there a lot of girls at the other facilities?"

He stopped in his tracks and turned to me. "No, only a few." He had this look on his face that made me think he was worried about my curiosity.

I frowned. "Are girls not allowed to be part of the program?"

His eyes worked across my face as if he tried to figure out a way to answer my question. "You ask so many questions." He smiled. "All of them will be answered at the end of camp."

I thought about the other girls. Why weren't they at the party? "You have five to choose from here."

"I have three."

"What about the other two?"

"They went home." He began walking.

I stood there, thinking. Everything seemed weird and I didn't like that he wouldn't explain any of it to me. So what if it was a secret and he would explain it later. I needed to know right now. "I think I should get back to Sarah."

He turned to me. I could tell by the light on his face he was frustrated with my questions. "Listen, Christa," he said as he came closer. "I want to tell you everything."

"Then do it."

"I can't." He took a breath. "There's a connection between us."

I knew that. I was drawn to him for some reason.

"I know you feel it and I don't want to scare you off before you get a chance to see what we do here."

That really helps. I felt so confused. "What are you saying?"

His palm slid along my arm sending the nerves into overdrive. "I want you to choose to be a part of this life. The life me and my family live."

I stared at his face. I wanted to tell him yes at that moment. I wanted the family he spoke of. I wanted to wrap my arms around him and press my lips to his but I couldn't. I didn't know anything about him or the facility. For all I knew, it was an occult. "I don't know," I mumbled.

"Don't decided yet, just think about it this week and when I stand in front of you and your friends and tell yons about my team, then decide."

I couldn't help but nod. One thing was for certain, we did have a connection. It was obvious the longer we were together. When I first met him, I thought it was a warning but now I realized it was a pull—a rubber band pulling us together. Well, at least I hoped it was a good thing because if it wasn't. It was too late for me.

Chapter 13

I didn't get the bad vibe from Carter as I did the other boys. For that reason, I trusted him. I honestly believed he wouldn't hurt me, so I followed him on.

"Where are you taking me?"

He smiled as we walked. "A waterfall. When the moon sits over it, it casts a glow on it. It's pretty amazing."

"Sounds beautiful."

The deeper we walked into the forest, a chill wiped through the air. From time to time, the breeze would cause me to shiver. Chill bumps erupted on my arms and I wished I had a sweatshirt on.

He stopped and looked at me. "Are you cold?" He glanced at his own clothes. "Of course you are." He didn't even wait for me to answer.

As I hugged myself, I admitted, "I'll be fine."

He wrapped his arm around me, pulling me in against him. The warmth of his body chased the chill away or maybe it was because I was blushing like a little girl again.

"We'll go back and I'll bring you out tomorrow."

I nodded but when we turned to go back a giggle broke the calmness. We looked behind us and stared in the direction it came from. He put a finger to his lips and turned the light off. Taking my hand, he led me into the darkness. My adrenaline pumped as we snuck up on the soft glow of a lantern at the base of the waterfall.

We hunkered down behind a boulder and peeked out at the couple in the water. My mouth fell open at Tony and Becca submerged in the liquid. Carter smiled at me then pulled me away from the moon bathers.

After we ran back down the trail toward the fire, he flipped the light back on and whispered, "I told you she liked him."

"I could see that." I really didn't want the image in my brain any longer.

"I didn't know they would be there," he said.

"It's OK."

He smiled lightly as he put his arm back around me. I wasn't going to tell him, I wasn't cold anymore. From the excitement and running my blood pumped through my body faster than before and I was good and toasty.

"I still want to see the falls."

A grin worked across his face that made me happy. "I'll come by your cabin at seven. We won't need a flashlight to get out here but I want you to see the moon shine on it."

I smiled at him. "Sounds good."

Orange flames danced in the distance, peeking from behind the trees and branches as we made our way back to the field. The music drifted through the night but not as loud as before. It was probably since most of the guest had called it a night. Ethan and Sarah were in the same spot. She leaned against him with a cup in her hand. I hoped he didn't force it on her.

"How old is Ethan?" I wondered.

"Eighteen."

Frowning I asked, "Are you the only ones?"

"No. Dean and Becca are the exceptions."

When we got closer to the fire, I called out, "Sarah are you ready to go?"

"Yes." She stood up and looked at Ethan. "Thank you for a great time."

He stood, pulling her into a hug. "Thank you for deciding to come."

I stared at her. "Have you been drinking?"

She laughed. "No, Mom. It's pop." She handed me the cup.

Carter and Ethan smiled at me for being weird, I guess. She was one of my best friends I was going to take care of her.

"We'll walk you to your cabin," Carter said as he motioned for Ethan and Sarah to go ahead.

At the corner of the cabin, a growl came from the trees at our left. I stopped and listen to the commotion taking place in the woods. It rolled across the night, sounding like a big mad cat deep in the forest.

"What was that?"

Carter took hold of mine and Sarah's arms and pulled us to the porch. "Let's get you inside." Ethan stood in the yard, fists clenched, looking into the darkness.

"What's going on?" I could sense the uneasiness that swarmed them.

He put on a smile that was different than any other I'd seen. "It's only a bobcat. There are a lot of them around here and the food brings them into camp." He sighed. "Would you check and see if Mandy's inside?"

I nodded and opened the cabin door. Sarah walked on inside as I glanced into the room. Mandy sat on the couch with Rob. "She is."

"Good, now you go inside." He frowned. "Let them know to stay inside for the rest of the night. I would hate for someone to come face to face with a big one." He took two steps away then stopped, turning slightly to look at me. "I'll see you tomorrow?"

I nodded. "Seven."

He smiled that heartwarming smile. "At seven."

I couldn't wait.

Chapter 14

The moment my head hit the pillow, I fell asleep.

The sounds of the Bobcats drifted into the cabin and I dreamed of them. My imagination made them bigger with a black coat and a long tail. It was as thick as my wrist, waving in and out of the branches. I knew bobcats didn't have tails so I wondered why I dreamed of them that way.

A woman stood in the darkness. Her pale skin made her glow like the moon. Her face was soft and friendly. She told me to trust Carter that he would protect me. A cat came from the darkness near her. Its eyes locked on me. He growled, showing long white teeth. She warned me, trying to get me to move but I couldn't understand her. It was as if she were a ghost trying to communicate using the energy in the air. Her mouth opened and closed as my eyes went from her to the cat and back. My heart raced as the animal moved closer. I was frozen with fear. My feet wouldn't move. Then it sprang.

I shot upright in bed. The sound of cats fighting tore through the night. Sometimes it sounded as if a woman was screaming at the top of her lungs. A chill ran down my spine, causing me to shake with each outburst. I'd never heard such a racket.

Pulling my blanket under my chin, I rolled over and faced the door. I was no stranger to the outdoors. I loved it but the commotion coming from the forest frightened me. I didn't know if I ever wanted to step foot in the woods again.

Luckily, after a while, the sounds died down and I drifted off to sleep.

When it was time to get up, the sun hadn't risen. I really didn't want to run the five miles in the dark after what took place a few hours ago. Dean waited for us at the trails start. He eyed his watch as we dragged ourselves into formation. I didn't understand how he could be bright-eyed and bushy-tailed after all the beer he'd drunk. He screamed at us and bombarded us with warm-ups. Our hearts were beating a steady rate when the sun made its daily debut. I was relieved the darkness wouldn't be accompanying us on our run.

Like the day before, Mandy and Rob were close on Dean's heels while Sarah and I lagged. I knew I could do better but I wasn't letting her fail.

Besides, Tony was in the same position as me—bringing up the rear.

"Come on, Sarah," I encouraged her, "You can run faster than this."

"I'm tired."

I knew if I wanted a shot at being a part of this group, I had to impress Dean. The only way I was doing that was to get Sarah moving. "Imagine Ethan's waiting for you at the finish line. The faster you get through the course, the longer you'll get to sit with him at breakfast."

She hit a new gear. She hurdled logs and ditches. I smiled at my victory since I could do my own thing. It took us thirty minutes to finish the run, shaving off ten minutes from yesterday. I was proud of myself for using my secret weapon on her and his name was Ethan.

"Way to pick it up, Sarah," Dean committed. "Tomorrow, Tony, I want you running with me. Let's see if you can't finish in under twenty."

Tony frowned. "Are you serious?"

"Becca runs it in fifteen."

His mouth fell open. "'Cause she likes it."

Dean smiled. "Go get some breakfast."

As I filled my plate, I scanned the tables for Carter. I couldn't help but notice Ethan wasn't anywhere to be seen either. Sitting down, I saw the disappointment on Sarah's face and I wanted to give her some support. "They're probably busy."

She smiled slightly with a nod.

"We didn't get to talk last night," Mandy began, "How was the party?"

Sarah stared at her eggs. "Fun."

"Carter's nice," I added.

"Did you get the scoop on this place?" Rob leaned across the table so the other patrons wouldn't hear our conversation.

"All I got was if we're still here by the end, all of our questions would be answered." I shrugged. "They're being secretive about it."

"Don't you think that's weird?" Rob asked.

I shrugged. "That's the only thing you think is weird about this place?"

He sighed as he looked around at the tables.

"I'll keep trying." They didn't like my answer but they went back to eating.

I leaned into Tony. "How was your night? You didn't get back till late."

He smiled. "Good."

I mumbled, "I bet."

He glared at me. "What's that supposed to mean?"

"Nothing," I admitted. "Just seen you and Becca on the dance floor then you disappeared."

He nodded. "She's not like anyone I've ever met before."

I believed he truly liked her. I'd seen him with girls before and he didn't act strange afterward. Something about Becca got him thinking.

It also got me to think. The girls, who were here, seemed like they were ready for a boyfriend. Was that the whole purpose of the camp or was I looking into it too hard? All I knew, I liked Carter and Sarah liked Ethan. Tony was into Becca. Was this why we were invited? I frowned at my thoughts and glanced around at my friends. *What is really going on here?*

Chapter 15

While my friends talked back and forth about the party and how much fun they had, I listened. I had agreed with them but the noise in the woods did it for me. It didn't help with the dream of the panther adding to it. As I thought of it, I wondered if they heard the commotion in the forest.

"Did any of you hear those cats last night?"

They shook their heads as if they had no clue what I was talking about. How did they not hear them? Did I just dream it all?

After breakfast, we took our hour break then went to the field behind the cabins for another day of self-defense training. I dreaded sparing with Becca. I really wasn't in the mood to be punched in the gut.

When we lined up next to Dean and Becca I was relieved to find fighting dummies waiting for us. They taught us how to punch correctly, then how to kick. After a few hours, we were panting and sweating as if we'd run a twenty-three mile marathon.

Becca stopped next to me for a minute and watched as I did my best one-two punch. She smiled and went on to observe Mandy.

Sarah came over. "Do you think it's weird that we're the only people training today?"

I shrugged. "Carter mentioned some of the others had left."

She frowned. "Why? Did they give up after a day?"

I shrugged and went back to punching my dummy. I couldn't tell her what he'd told me. Could I? He told it to me in confidence.

Three more hours of running, ropes, push-ups and crunches and we were off to dinner. It wasn't long until Carter was supposed to meet me at the cabin. I still hadn't seen him or Ethan. It made me wonder what they had to do that kept them away for so long.

Sarah and I were first on the shower schedule, so when we finished our dinner we hurried back to the cabin to get ready for later. Sarah had high hopes that Ethan would stop by so she wanted to be ready just in case.

I decided to wear jeans. Since I got cold the night before, I didn't want to take the chance tonight. I slipped on another tee-shirt and hoped my hair didn't have any flyaways. Then I paced the floor waiting for the clock to hit seven. With each twist in the next direction, my heart raced a little more.

The door hinges groaned, alerting me to someone opening the front door. I jerked around as I sucked in a breath of anticipation. Rob and Mandy walked inside. I slouched, from the disappointment, and exhaled.

Mandy eyed me. "Expecting someone?"

I nodded as I tried not to eat my lip.

"When?"

"Seven."

It was ten 'till.

She smiled. "You still got some time."

I sighed. My heart thumped loud enough Mandy could hear it from across the room. I paced, trying to do something other than pulling my hair out because I wanted to scream. What if he stands me up? What if he didn't want to see me again?

A knock erupted on the door and I froze. Rob strolled over, an amused look on his face. He opened the door but only enough he could see out. "Hey, Carter."

"Rob. How are you?"

"Good. What can I do for you?"

I couldn't help the smile that stretched across my face. Rob acted like he was my dad and I liked it. It made me feel special. I'd never had anyone do that for me before.

"Christa and I are going for a walk."

Mandy looked at me and mouthed, *Christa...*

I took a deep breath, forcing myself to not look as if this was the best day of my life because it was. When I got to the door, butterfly's danced in my tummy. My heart felt as if it were going to burst. I chewed on my lip to keep from grinning from ear to ear. Instead, I looked him from head to toe; jeans, boots and an Army tee. *How was he so perfect?*

I stepped through the door. "Ready?" Carter asked.

I nodded and took his waiting hand.

As we walked across the field, I tried to pull together enough courage to talk to him. It was hard to think of something when you didn't want to sound stupid. I wanted him to know I was smart, not the hillbilly, white trash most people saw me as.

"I haven't seen you all day."

"I had something to take care of."

I glanced at him. "Ethan too?"

"It was our responsibility." He glanced back.

My eyes drifted over the thick shrubbery, growing along the path. I even got a whiff of a flower from time to time. It kind of reminded me of honeysuckle.

"Sarah thinks he was only being nice because he felt sorry for her."

"No," he said with a smile. "He likes her. Drove me nuts talking about her all day."

I smiled. It made me happy to know Sarah was getting what she wanted.

We walked along the trail, enjoying the scenery. Big trees with wide canopies shielded us from the sun. Birds flew around, calling out in their own song. The sound of water running pulled you toward the hidden beauty that you could imagine hid behind the rocks. We stepped up on a bank and saw the fifteen-foot wide waterfall.

The water trickled over the edge with a steady stream. It wasn't a thick heavy stream—a slow pour. Large green ivy bushes with big pink blossoms grew around black rocks. Tall beach trees shaded the stream but allowed some light to drift through the branches. Rocks glistened as the water ran over them and poured into a pool of blues and greens before it stretched on downstream.

Carter stepped across a small bank onto a boulder. It sat half in the water. He reached out his hand to help me across. I took it, as I imagined sitting on the rock, sunbathing.

"Wow." I turned, staring at the beauty around me. "It's beautiful."

"Yes, it is." He sat down. "I've always liked it here."

I took in the scenery as I sat next to him. I loved the forest, everything about it. It was pure and natural. *Even the scary parts*, I thought.

I frowned at myself for thinking it. It was as if it weren't my thoughts but someone else's.

"What happened with the Bobcats?"

He glanced at me, a form of surprise in his eyes. "Nothing."

"I tried to sleep but all I could hear was this awful racket like they were fighting," I told him.

He leaned back on his elbows. "You don't have to worry about them anymore."

I thought of my crazy dream—the strange woman and the panther. It made me question what was truly in the woods. "Are you sure they were bobcats?"

He smiled. "What else would it have been?"

I traced a crack in the rock next to me as I thought about how to answer it. "When I looked in the tree last night, I saw something." I looked at him, meeting his eyes. "I saw a panther."

Chapter 16

I let what I said sink in. He didn't seem as if my acknowledgment bothered him. It did me. Why would he lie about what was in the woods? I know that was what it was. Why else would I have dreamed of them?

"It could've been." He shrugged. "There are all kinds of animals in these woods." He smiled. "Don't worry about them though, you're safe with me."

I stared at him, trying to read him. I wanted to not trust him but it was the total opposite. I felt safe with him. It was such a foreign feeling to me. My entire life I'd had to build these walls to keep myself safe. I didn't have the pleasure of getting it from someone else.

He took my silence as a denial. Taking my hand, he added, "I promise, I won't let anything happen to you."

My heartbeat picked up. As I looked into his baby blues, I tried to not let it control me. I needed to get a grip on the feelings he caused to stir in me. *Focus,* I told myself.

So I changed the subject instead. "How long have you been in the Army?"

"Six months."

That's all? "Tell me about your family."

He laughed. "We talked about them last night." He smiled. "Tell me about yours."

I frowned. I didn't want to tell him about my home life. I knew it was common to be in my position but some people saw it as being bad. He had a wonderful family. It intimidated me.

"OK." He said, "Let me ask you this…"

I frowned. "What?"

"You won't talk about your family, I get it. Will you tell me why you want to join the service?" His voice became soft. "Everyone has their own reasons."

"What makes you think I'd tell you the truth?"

He cocked his head to the side. "A hunch." He thought. "You want me to guess?"

I shrugged, wondering if he could read me.

"You only have a few people in the military, different categories," he started. "You got people who are just into the idea of drawing a weapon on someone." He stared at me.

"Am I a killer?"

"No," he answered fast. "Ones who believe it was their duty because a family member had already paid the price or was enlisted."

"Am I following in Daddy's footsteps?"

"No." He took a breath. "Patriot?"

His fingers slide along my fingers. I stared at him, hoping he didn't ask me the one question I didn't want him to know. My breathing picked up as my body flushed with heat.

"Family?"

There it was. I hoped I hadn't given the answer away. It was my business.

He inhaled and scooted closer to me. His body shielded the few rays of sun that drifted through the tree branches onto my face.

"I'm not going to push you, Christa. When you're ready to talk about anything, everything… I'll be right here."

I appreciated it. How could he make me feel so special when he talked to me? No one tried to. Not even a counselor, the DFS agent or foster parent.

I took a deep breath and leaned against him. He let me put my weight on him as I watched a leaf fall from a low hanging branch. I slowly fell into the water and drifted off downstream.

"This facility is a part of my family," he said, "I handpicked each of them because I saw them as a brother. Ethan is my best friend; I've known him since we were two." He laughed as if he remembered something that happened then. "Remember when I told you I ran the camp?"

I nodded. "It's your birthright." His words, not mine.

"This is my family and I want you to be a part of it." He looked down at me. "I want you to stay, to consider being one of my female cadets."

I swallowed the lump that was trying to rise into my throat. How could I answer that? I wanted to stay, to continue to get the attention I was from him. But I was fifteen. I wasn't ready to commit to a boy, to say I'd be his forever. Because when I did, it was going to be until I died.

"I'm having fun with you, Carter."

He laughed. "I'm not asking you to marry me."

I frowned as my face flushed. "I didn't think you were but I'm not going to agree to be a part of your camp because I like you." I quickly diverted my eyes from his face.

"You like me?" His voice sounded as if that made him happy.

I wasn't going to get out of this. I'd already stuck my big foot in my mouth. "I only said what you did last night. We have a connection." I couldn't deny that and I believed everyone around us knew of it too.

He nodded, softly. "I'm not asking you to decide now. Besides you don't know everything."

"Exactly," I added, "I'm beginning to think you run an occult."

He laughed which loosened me up. "No. We aren't an occult."

I laughed at my own stupidity. I sighed as I got back in the comfortable spot under his arm. He hugged me against him. One thing was for sure, there would always be an adventure. I would also have a huge family. As I took a deep breath, filling my lungs with nature, I told him, "I'll consider it."

Chapter 17

When Carter walked me back to the cabin, after dark, Sarah and Ethan were nowhere to be seen. He assured me she was perfectly safe. I had my doubts but took his word and allowed him to push me through the door with a smile I could die for.

Five am came fast.

I felt as if I'd just lain down when Rob's phone buzzed a wake-up call. It hadn't helped, I couldn't sleep. I waited for Sarah to come home. She did about an hour after me. Everyone was in their bunks but not asleep. She ignored Tony's teasing and went to get ready for bed.

When I knew she was safe, I still kept thinking of what Carter had said. I tried to look at the bad side of the camp but I couldn't. Maybe I was naive in thinking they could be my family. I wanted one so bad that I didn't care about the cost.

As Dean called out our warm-ups, I did my best to follow along. It was as if I were in a daze the entire time. I was worried about the run. Sarah and I were going to be in the back while Tony ran alongside Dean. It was my responsibility to get Sarah motivated and focused on finishing the course in a timely manner.

"Tony, you run with me. Rob, Mandy, keep up the good work. Chris, I think you can do better. Sarah keep up with Chris." He took off down the path and we followed.

The first hundred feet of trail shot downhill. Shoes and rain wore the path down to where it was slick even though it was dry. When you sucked in a breath, it was the dirt we scattered about. Every other step, you had to jump over a root protruding from the ground. At the bottom was a small creek. It was a ten-foot section of water joined by two hills. It was deep enough to get your feet wet with small pebbles along the bed. You had to take two good breaths before the trail started up the next hill.

Sarah started up the three-foot embankment but the loose dirt caused her to slip. I quickly braced myself letting her use my knee for a foothold so she could get up. The moment she was standing, I climbed up. At the top of the hill, I got a strange feeling. It was as if someone watched me. I'd always felt as if the forest had eyes, watching my every movement but this was different. It was eerie almost. Looking around, I saw Rob and Mandy's backs as they disappeared around the bend and Sarah a few feet in front of me but no one else.

Shrugging the uneasiness away, I hurried to catch up with Sarah. The woods around us quieted, making the hairs on my arm to stand to attention. A twig broke behind me. I jerked around. A fist flew at my face. It was so sudden I had no time to react. The impact sent me to the ground. I groaned as tears filled my eyes. A muffled scream made me push to get up. *Sarah*, I thought. Feet scrambled in the leaves around me and then a second punch knocked me out.

***

A dull ache shot through my head. My cheek throbbed worse than a toothache. Rolling over, I dug my fingers into the cool dirt. I groaned and pried my eyes open to see where I was.

"Chris," Sarah whispered next to me.

Sitting back on my knees, I turned to her voice. She was balled in the corner of a makeshift cage. My eyes darted around the cell. The two back walls were rock and the front was a large metal wall that reminded me of a cell door. It smelled like a wet basement and a tunnel led out to a light source. I swallowed with the realization we were in a cave. *Home sweet home*, I thought.

"Do you know where we are?" I rose and began pulling at the metal beams.

"They blindfolded me."

They didn't punch you in the face? The thought made me pause. *Why did they hit me?*

I jerked on the door but it wouldn't budge so I kicked it and instantly wished I hadn't when the pain that shot up my leg was worse than the pain in my face.

Taking a breath, I turned back to Sarah, "Who is it?"

"I don't know but there's more than two."

I assumed. Now I had to figure out who it was.

Sighing, I sat next to Sarah. I needed to think, to try and get us out of here. I stared at a small candle that sat on a rock. It gave us enough light to see by. The rotten odor of earth made me want to sneeze. Noises echoed from the outside of the cave. I glanced at the exit where the sun cast a yellow hue on the world. A figure entered, blocking the light outside. I scooted next to Sarah and put my arm around her shoulders.

The shadow seemed to fill with color revealing a boy. He walked up to the cell. "Wakey, wakey," he sang.

He was shorter and thinner than most boys around the camp. As I stared at him something stood out. He looked familiar to me. "What do you want?"

"We want you and," he pointed to Sarah, "You."

She cringed and I made sure to put myself in front of her. "Who's helping you?" He wasn't getting anywhere near us.

He laid his head against the bars. "I'm going to enjoy what comes next."

"You're not doing anything," a familiar voice called out.

My eyes widened as Greg came out of the tunnel into the room. His buddies from the bomb fire followed close behind. When I glanced at the first one, I remembered he was the one who stood in the back and laughed like a little girl when they came over to me.

"Hello, Sarah, Chris. It's good to see you both again."

My breath came fast as I tried to slow my heart rate. "It's not for us."

He came closer, looking me over. "Sorry 'bout your face." Turning to the others, he said, "They are the start of our Pride. According to a high ranking official, they are willing to give me whatever I want if I can prove Carter and his Pride aren't fit to be part of the Army anymore." He paced slowly. "They want the Rollins' out of the picture and this is how we do it." He turned to me and Sarah.

A smile spread across his face that made me want to turn and run but I had nowhere to go. I was trapped.

He looked at his buddies. "Behave. When we get to our new home, then we will decide who gets who." He took a breath. "Let's get back; we got a search party to attend." Greg glanced over his shoulder at me. "Apparently, you wandered off the trail."

The only thing I could think of was what Carter had said. He promised he would take care of me, protect me. It scared me though. What if he did come? By the look on Greg's face, it was exactly what he wanted.

Greg took hold of one of the bars while the others walked out into the light. He stared at Sarah then me. "Don't worry 'bout your friends. They won't be hurt." Without another word, he ran after his buddies, leaving Sarah and me alone in a dimming cave.

Chapter 18

Time dragged by.

The candle that sat on the rock burnt down until it was a flicker. It bowed each time a breeze slipped into the opening of the cave. Wax melted down on the stone in an odd pattern. It resembled a silhouette of a face: hollow eyes, skeleton nose and a beard.

I didn't move as the darkness hugged us in a heavy blanket. Even though my eyelids felt heavy, I stared at the orange flame. A rat scurried across the floor and I jerked from the surprise but continued to watch. Insects called out and I said an inner prayer for nothing else to show up unannounced.

Sarah slept.

When Greg left, she cried. I held her until the whimpers faded and her body relaxed. I was glad she could sleep because I wasn't closing my eyes. I wanted to see them coming.

My eyes felt heavier with each heartbeat. The darkness weighed them, causing me to nod off from time to time. I constantly shook my head and pried my lids open, refusing to let sleep win. I needed to be ready.

A roar shrieked through the cave, causing me to jerk upright. My heart hammered to a beat of a rapid drum. A growl rolled into the room. It was as if the sound was magnified by the walls, pulsating inward toward us. From the darkness, two eyes appeared. The small flame of the candle danced in the reflection, focused on me. I sucked in a breath as the panther came forward. A black cat that was bigger than most dogs with a tail as long as I was tall, paced in front of the cage. His head was lowered and each time he turned, a rumble began deep in his belly and escaped his lips. It reminded me of the tigers at the zoo, watching, waiting for their prey.

The cat stopped mid-stride. His head turned to the door and in walked Greg as if the panther standing in front of him was his house pet. My eyes went from Greg to the cat and back again. My mouth was a jar. *What's happening?*

"Carter's getting close," he talked as if I cared what he had to say. "I gotta do something to throw him off your trail." He moved to the cage and stood next to the door with his hands on his hips, staring at me. "Come here."

I shook my head. I wasn't getting anywhere near that animal, either of them.

A smirk covered his face. "If you don't come here, I'll let him in there." He sighed. "With Sarah."

I glanced over at her. She was sleeping as if she hadn't heard a sound. I had to protect her so I eased off the dirt and went to the door where Greg stood. He reached through the bars and grabbed a handful of my shirt and jerked. The hem ripped up to my ribcage, showing my belly. His eyes lingered there for a moment then he smiled. I wanted to vomit. He made me sick.

Turning to the panther, he held the piece of my shirt out and said, "Lead Carter into the next territory. I want him to think his Rivals took his Pride females."

That was what, the third time he had said that word. *Pride.*

Images of the panther in my dreams, the sounds of the cats fighting and the one that just left…it all made sense now. It was a cat's Pride. I felt stupid for not seeing it sooner. With the recognition, a weight lifted from me. Thinking about some of the things Carter said, it made sense. They are Recon. I wanted to laugh at myself. No one in their right mind would expect a team of Panthers to work for the military.

How? I wondered. Where did they come from? I never believed werewolves or vampires were real. They were a Hollywood creature but witches. I believed witches existed, especially the ones who used nature to their benefit. Could believing in them help me accept what was in front of me more easily?

"Let Sarah go." I tried to get him to focus on me. "I'm the only one you need."

He smiled. "I know you want to protect your friend." He walked over to the opposite side of the room. "I already got her so I'm gonna keep her."

I disliked not being in control. The last time I was in a situation like this—a bad home with locked doors everywhere—I swore I'd never let it happen again. My heartbeat picked up. My breathing grew erratic. I didn't like how he made me feel. The fear, I had.

I grabbed the bars. "Let us out of here," I called through gritted teeth as I shook the bars.

His eyes widened from my outburst then he went to the opening and picked up a backpack that I didn't see him drop when he came in. I was too busy worried about a panther wanting to eat me for lunch. He pulled out two bottles of water and handed them to me. I took them. Then he held out two sandwiches.

I glanced at his arm stuck through the bars. Sitting the bottles down, I grabbed his wrist and twisted his arm around to where his face was pressed into the metal. "Let us out," I growled.

A roar that made ever tiny hair on my body stand at attention came into the cave with the panther. I eyed the black cat then Greg.

"She's just playing," Greg said, "Aren't you, Chris?"

I twisted harder, hoping he would give up and let us out.

"If he hears a bone crack, he will attack." He shook his head. "He doesn't care if you are a girl."

At least I was in the cage and he couldn't get in, I thought. I wanted to smile but then I realized we would never get out. He would be right there waiting for us. It was hopeless.

The cat stepped closer, his eyes locked on me, ears pinned back. My heart raced, fueling my adrenaline.

"Chris," Greg warned.

I didn't have a choice. If they did open the gate, the panther would tear me to shreds and I wasn't about to leave Sarah here alone. Not where no one knew where we were.

I let go. Greg rolled his shoulder as I stepped back out of his reach. Narrowing his eyes at me, he said, "If you ever do that again, I will beat you black and blue."

I didn't say anything. I just watched the man who I believed would beat me to death, turn away.

"I'll be back in the morning." He glanced at the panther. "Troy'll keep you company." He walked out of the cave.

I stared at Troy. He paced in front of the cage and all that I could think of was, *why me*?

Chapter 19

Before I settled down next to Sarah, I retrieved the water and the sandwiches. I took a swig and hoped I wouldn't have to pee anytime soon because I wasn't doing it in front of the cat. There was something in his eyes that was unnerving.

I tried to sit more in front of Sarah, that way in case I fell asleep and she moved I would wake up. Even though I tried to not visit dreamland, I did.

I dreamed of panthers, of a woman and a man. They were a couple, a king and queen, with crowns on their heads. Panthers surrounded them as if they were their guards. Their coats black as night, teeth white as the snow. Growls filled my head, reverberating through my body.

I wasn't afraid of them. I wanted to be closer.

As if I was there, I stepped forward. Closer I moved until one panther stepped forward. Hunkering down, he came within reach. The light of the candles, slid across his coat showing a faint detail like printed silk. His eyes were a bright blue like an autumn sky. I stared into his eyes. They were calm and exhilarating. Reaching out, I wanted to touch him, to feel if his coat was as soft as it seemed to be. However, when my fingers were about to make contact, he crouched, letting out a roar that caused me to jerk back.

I sat up. My skin dripped with perspiration. The beat of my heart thumped so hard I thought I would pass out. I brushed my hair back out of my face and pulled my hair back up into a ponytail. I looked up to see two boys sitting with a panther and I was the center of their attention.

Sarah stirred. Her eyes worked around the cave then she sat up. "I hoped I was dreaming."

I sighed then muttered, "You and me both."

When her eyes took in the panther, they widened. "Oh gosh."

"Yeah." I wasn't ready to tell her I thought they were all shifters.

As I sat there, sipping my water, I replayed the dream in my head. It was strange. In a way, it was as if I knew them, trusted them, but I didn't know why. How could I feel that way? I didn't know anyone who was royalty. I laughed at myself for thinking the queen and king were the weirdest things in my dream. It still made me wonder why was I dreaming about them now?

"Chris," Sarah whispered, as she hugged her knees to her body. "I have to pee."

I'd hoped we would've been out of this before we'd thought about the bathroom. Unfortunately, when she told me, my own bladder reacted. "Me too."

I stood and looked around the cave. There was no bathroom to be seen so I figured they would let us go outside. "Hey," I called. "We need to use the bathroom." I felt stupid for asking but what else was I supposed to say. We need to use the bushes.

The big guy who had no hair and never spoke a word came over. He pointed to the back of the cave. "Use the can."

"Excuse me?" Did they really expect us to drop our drawers in front of them? "I'm not using a can."

Balling my hands into fists, I wanted to punch them. This was so wrong on so many levels. I turned to Sarah. Her eyes were red and she stared into the cave as if she had no thought.

Sighing, I turned back to them. "Can we at least have some privacy?"

The big guy turned toward the cat and then the panther marched the boys out into the forest. As I watched them disappear, I realized the panther was Greg. After all, he was their leader.

After we were finished, the boys came back in and Greg took up his place pacing in front of the cage door. I cuddled up with Sarah and tried to push the realization away that with each hour that past, we weren't getting out of this. Yet I forced myself to believe we could. We had to.

I didn't know how long we sat in the dirt, watching the dumbasses play cards. We did what we could to pass the time but dozing off seemed to work better. I dreamed of Carter. I felt safe with him but when I opened my eyes, I was back in hell.

More time ticked by. I leaned against the rock; the coolness seemed to sink into my body, holding me still. I stared at the dirt, listening to the sounds around me. There was a drip that echoed in the stone. I glanced up at the ceiling, wondering where the water came from. *Drip...Drip...* It was hypnotizing.

Greg, the panther, shot from the cavern without warning. I rose up to see a third boy come into the cave with the cat. He was breathing heavily, bent at the waist with his hands on his knees.

"They believe the Rivals took them," he began, "Dean sent for backup. Mitch will be here tonight."

"We need to move them before Mitch gets here," the big man said, "he's smart. He'll see straight through the diversion."

The panther made some noises as if he spoke to each of the boys. I watched, wondering what they were going to do. And who was Mitch?

The new guy nodded. "He thinks you and Troy went back to Fort Knox."

Troy glared at me. "I think we should just use them for a little fun and get out of here."

"They're not dogs, you dick." The big guy glared at him.

Greg roared. The sound sent chills through me, causing the fine hairs all over my body to stand at attention. Sarah began to shake. They looked at the panther and nodded with clenched jaws.

"Do you want me to knock her out again?" Troy smiled as he glanced over at me.

I stiffened. He punched me. That little Wessel was the one who knocked me out. My hands balled into fists as my eyes narrowed at him. One thing I would do was make him pay for what he did to me.

The new guy started undressing. Sarah grabbed my hand. I swallowed, as I realized he was going to change right in front of us. Sarah turned her face and buried it against my shoulder. I didn't blame her. She refused to see what would happen but I was curious. I wanted to know if it was true. Would he really turn into a panther?

He pulled off his pants and kneeled down on the dirt. His skin started to roll and move as if he had bugs crawling under his skin. The sounds of cracking bones and cartilage realigning echoed against the walls. My eyes widened as I watched his hands and feet shifted into paws. His human legs and arms formed into powerful legs of the panther. Next, his face stretched, widened and transformed into the cat. Then his spine extended, lengthening into a thick, long tail. In one last shudder, the hair erupted over his skin, leaving nothing left of the boy who ran into the cave moments ago.

I couldn't move. My heart thumped so loud it drowned out all sound. My eyes felt as if they were filled with sand as I stared at the end result. I didn't know if I wanted to believe what I witnessed. It was true, though. These boys and this camp were all Panthers and it was why they wanted new members. They wanted to change us all into panthers but only if we wanted it.

I tried to take a breath to calm my nerves. How was this possible? I finally blinked. *Now what,* I thought.

"Keep them distracted while we take them over the mountain," Baldy said.

In one bound, the new panther fled from the cave.

Troy smiled, devilishly, as he eyed me and Sarah. "Hey, Bob, let me have the little one."

Bob glanced at Greg as if asking permission then came to the door with a rope. Troy followed. He leaned against the bars and made kissing noises while Bob unlocked the big chain.

I wanted to throw up. He was the definition of a sleazy pervert.

When the door opened, Greg came in. Sarah recoiled from the panther coming closer. I didn't back away; I sat still, trying to keep myself in front of Sarah. I sat taller as Greg came almost nose to nose with me. It didn't matter that he was a lethal predator. I wasn't moving. He would have to kill me to get to Sarah.

Troy reached for Sarah but I knocked his hand away. "You will not lay a hand on her." I made sure my tone told them I wasn't playing.

Troy laughed but Bob stepped by him to help Sarah from the ground. I took one more glance at Greg then I stood. The maggot who thought it was fun to punch girls was the center of my attention now.

As Bob tied the rope around her hands, her eyes filled with tears. "Chris?" she whispered.

I felt awful. I didn't know how to help her. I was in the same boat. "It's OK. I'll be right behind you."

I watched as Bob helped Sarah out of the cage and down the tunnel. Troy came forward and Greg growled a warning. It made me realize something. Greg wanted me in one piece, something that was to my advantage. As Troy tied the rope around my hands, I had an inner smile. Now, he would deal with me.

Chapter 20

Troy left a good three feet between us on the rope he led me with. When he stepped out of the cell, he jerked the slack which caused me to stumble. My knees planted into the pea-sized rocks. The fiery pain caused me to grit my teeth. I automatically wished I had run in sweats so I wouldn't have skinned my knees. Troy was impatient and pulled at my restraints while I was down. The force caused the rope to dig into my wrists, sending a burning sensation into my arms.

When I stood, Greg ran down the tunnel and into the sun. The moment the sun hit my face, I shielded my eyes from the brightness. Then I took a look at where we were. I sucked in a breath from the view. We were standing on the side of a mountain. I say mountain but it wasn't like the big mountains with white peaks or rolling gray stone. We were in Kentucky. The mountains here were thick with woods. Looking down, it was like a climbing wall for the advanced climber overlooking a sea of treetops. I looked up to see Bob helping Sarah up the cliff. They had the help of a rope that was tied to something at the top about two hundred feet above us.

Troy pulled me to the gap. I automatically took my hand-hold, then a foot-hold, following him up the mountain. The rocks were smooth in places where they had climbed up and down the hill. Even the dirt was caked into the cracks and hardened as if someone had trampled over it a few dozen times. My muscles tried to object to the weight they held but I sucked in all my motivations and pushed on.

At the top, I glanced behind me to see nothing but trees and rolling hills. It was if we were in the middle of nowhere, which we kind of were. The Appalachians were vast and wide. I pulled in a deep breath to ease my racing heart. The scent of muscadines filled my nose. It had been years seen I smelled the fruity, tart grape.

Once again, Troy didn't like me making him wait so he jerked on the rope. The force caused me to stumble. As I pulled in another breath, I thought about screaming but was it worth the risk. What were the odds someone was nearby? Instead, I focused on Troy and waited for my chance to get out of it on my own.

Greg led us deeper into the forest. I kept looking left and right to see if anything stood out. I tried to think about the maps we had read during training. How the land laid, the saddles, ridges and valleys. I knew the facility was at the bottom of two hills, so I knew I had to go down. I knew the cliffs were on the western side of the property. If they were worried about someone finding us then if I went down my chances were better than average at running into someone.

My dilemma was Sarah. Could I leave her? I didn't want to but I felt as if this was our only chance. If I didn't go, Carter's group would never find us. The good thing was, Troy was the evil one and in a way, he was coming with me because I knew he wouldn't let me go easily.

One thing was certain, I had to try.

You can do this, I thought.

I took a couple of deep breaths as I waited for my moment. Greg leaped over a fallen tree, disappearing into the underbrush. Bob lifted Sarah up over it next. We were a good fifty feet behind them. I twisted the rope into my hands. With each step, I gripped the braid and rolled it around my hands. When I had most of the slack, I jerked Troy toward me.

Troy stumbled backward. I brought my knee up into his gut as his momentum made it a harder hit. When he bowed, I brought my elbow down on the top of his head. He dropped the rope to clutch his head and then I reared back and pretended his head was a soccer ball. When he went down, I ran.

Winding the access rope into my hands, I pushed harder than I'd ever pushed my legs before in my life. I saw a gap and shot toward it. My breath came hard and fast but when Troy groaned, I gulped and dug down as deep as I could to make myself run faster.

Run! Shot through my head, because I knew he was coming. He was running but I had to be faster. *Run!*

I lowered my gaze and focused on the finish line. I had to be first. Barreling over the cliff, sticks and briars ripped at my bare legs. As I slid over the hill, it was hard to stay balanced but I pushed. In two bounds, I was over the hill, sliding in wet leaves at the bottom. I didn't dare turn to see if Troy was behind me. I didn't have to look to know he was. If I took one second, it could be my last.

I ran so hard my lungs felt like they would burst. My legs ached but I kept going. I focused on finding someone, anyone. I pushed through an ivy bush and the sound of running feet grew behind me.

Run! I wanted to scream at myself, to kick my own but for being slow. My heart was in my throat. I was tired but my adrenaline pushed me. Fueled me. Then I heard a familiar sound and smelled the sweetest scent.

The waterfall.

I was close. Barreling through the next bushes, my feet hit a trail. Feet pounded into the ground behind me. The thump grew louder with each step. Then as if out of thin air, his body collided with my back.

I lost my balance and fell forward. My face hit the dirt, sliding a few feet with his weight pressing me into the ground. I tried to take a breath but dirt and sweat smothered me. I swung my arms, trying to get him off of me so I could breathe. He grabbed my right arm and jerked me over onto my back. Air filled my lings instantly.

"Stupid bitch," he said, as he struggled to keep me still.

I kicked at him as he pulled me from the ground. He drew his fist back and let it fly. I dodged, bringing my knee up into his groin. He tightened his grip on my upper arm causing me to flinch. He groaned and punched me in the mouth. An explosion of blood poured on to my tongue. The taste of pennies filled my mouth as I fell backward with him on top of me. He straddled me but I kept kicking, bucking, whatever I could to get him off of me. I wasn't giving up that easy.

A low rumble came from the woods. My heart sank as the sound of the cat calmed Troy's movements. He looked up, over us. His eyes widened, as his grip loosened. If this was my last chance, I'd rather die being eaten by a panther then have Troy touch me. I kneed him and swung my clenched fists at his face. My combined fists hit him in the nose with a thump. He gripped his face. Blood poured between his fingers as he held his nose and rolled to the side off me.

Scrambling to my feet, I backed away from him. My heart raced as I slowly turned to my fate. A panther stood on the trail in front of me. As I stared at him, I knew it wasn't Greg. He looked different.

This panther was a beautiful color of black and red and his eyes were as blue as an autumn sky. Tears filled my eyes as I fell to my knees in front of him.
"Carter," I whispered.

Chapter 21

As tears blurred my vision, he gradually stepped toward me. Slowly, he let his fur slid against my shoulder. I lifted my hands to his neck and buried my fingers into his thick coat. Tears fell and he licked my face. He wanted to let me know he was there for me. I wanted to curl around him and cry but I couldn't. I had to get back to Sarah.

Troy groaned behind me, causing Carter to look up. I turned and watched him rub his hand across his face. I lifted the rope to my teeth and pulled at the knot, freeing myself.

"Greg and Bob have Sarah." He glanced at me. "Greg's like you…a panther." I wasn't sure if that was the right term. "Bob's with Sarah." Carter growled as he looked at Troy. "They said something about going over the mountain."

Carter glanced at me then walked toward Troy. He didn't hesitate, putting one big paw on his chest. He let out a roar which caused fine hairs on my arms to rise. Dropping the rope, I walked over and stood next to Carter and Troy. Within seconds, black panthers emerged from the forest.

From the direction of the field, Dean ran up behind me. His eyes were wide when he saw me. "Chris? What happened?" His eyes went to Carter and then to Troy. "Greg?" His eyes narrowed from the acknowledgment.

I nodded. "Sarah's with him."

The panther on Carter's right let out a growl that started in his stomach and rolled out through clenched teeth. I didn't have to be one of them to know who he was. *Ethan.* He was worried about Sarah.

"She's OK, Ethan," I told him so he wouldn't worry. "Bob's taking care of her." I looked at Troy. "Troy's the one who likes to hit girls," I said, as I touched my lip.

Carter growled then Dean asked, "Did Troy do that to your face?"

My mouth tasted of blood and dirt. Small pieces of grit were packed against my gums. "Yeah." I spit what I could get out. A bottle of water would be nice.

Carter growled directly in Troy's face as his claws extended. Troy jerked as Carter added more weight to the paw on his chest. Troy didn't say anything; he just laid there with his eyes the size of donuts.

I turned to Dean. "Are you going after Sarah?"

Dean glanced at Carter. "You said they were going over the mountain?" I nodded as a few other Panthers let out growls and noises as if they were talking. "The old mines."

I wondered if they were talking to one another. If they were discussing what to do next?

"Carter, Ethan, Joe and Randy will follow your scent back to where you split from them. Derrick, me and you will lock up Troy."

I refused by shaking my head. "I'm going after Sarah."

"It's too dangerous."

"Don't," I warned Dean. "Those assholes abducted me and held me hostage…in a cage and Sarah's with them." I took a breath. "I'm going back for her whether you like it or not."

Dean narrowed his eyes at Carter and I hoped he was standing up for me.

"Fine," he said, as he picked up my discarded rope. He flipped Troy over so he could tie his hands at the small of this back. Dean wasn't gentle as he pressed his knee between his shoulders and knotted the braid against his flesh.

"How are my friends?"

"Worried."

"Let 'em know we're OK."

He nodded. "Becca'll tell them."

I thought of all the right hooks Becca showed me. "If it wasn't for her, I wouldn't be standing here."

When Dean pulled Troy to standing, he gave me a worried look. "You shouldn't be going." I wanted to scream. "But Carter's the boss."

I looked down at Carter and let my hand slide from the top of his head to his back. He leaned into my leg, making me smile.

"Stay next to him."

"I will."

The others took off in a sprint with Ethan leading the way. I took a breath and tried to follow Carter. They disappeared into the underbrush without a sound. As I ran, I tried to go all out but it was intimidating. I had a panther running next to me as if he was out for a nice Sunday stroll. Even though it was hard, I pushed forward.

The path I made stood out with broken branches, ruffled leaves and shoe prints. When we reached the gap, I stopped. My eyes worked up the eighty percent grade hill. *How in the world*, I thought. Shaking my head, I took a deep breath and started climbing.

I ran and climbed up the bank. Leaves that were old, wet and combined with mud made me slide. I dug my toes into small crevasses trying to get enough traction to help me advance but it was hard. Reaching above me, I wrapped my fingers around a root. As I pulled myself up, my foot slipped and I hung mid-air for a moment until I regained my footing. Carter made a weird noise as he paced at the top. Taking a calming breath, from thinking I was about to tumble to the bottom, I forced all my energy into climbing the rest of the hill. I crawled and clawed my way up and over the top onto level ground.

At the top, Carter leaned against me. "Maybe I shouldn't have come." He snorted, nudging me with his nose.

Taking a deep breath, I stood. "OK," I said and took off after him.

Chapter 22

On the other side of the ridge, the woods became dense with shrubs and fallen trees. It was hard to keep up with Carter as he slipped underneath logs and through the underbrush. I had to climb over and go around most of it. When I climbed over a pine that was a victim of the winter's ice storm, Ethan startled me. He emerged from the bushes in front of us without a sound.

Carter stood stone still as Ethan looked around then headed back the way he'd come. The way they acted, we were close to Greg and Bob. It made me wish I could talk to him. I wanted to know what was going on. *Was Sarah OK?*

Carter watched Ethan slip away then turned toward me. He latched onto the hem of my shorts and pulled me with him. He stopped at a large laurel bush that had thin brown limbs that grew up and out. He glanced inside the shrub then at me. I got the message and climbed inside. He stood there watching as I got comfortable. Who knew how long I'd have to stay here or why I had to. It was irritating that I couldn't go. Did he not trust me? I could defend myself.

As soon as I was finished complaining in my head, I looked up. It was strange having a panther stare at you; however, he wasn't just a panther. He was Carter. His eyes revealed it all. In his blue orbs, I saw who he truly was and I felt safe in his gaze. He stepped forward, allowing me to slide my fingers along his jaw. He leaned into my touch. I believed it was his way of telling me he was happy because I was safe. His touch made me feel that way.

When I was about to ask him not to go, he backed out of the bush. He turned and disappeared into the next thicket. Thick leaves and underbrush swallowed him instantly. My heart sank at the feeling he was gone but then his head popped out. He snorted at me and I smiled. I knew what he was saying without the words. "I'll stay," I whispered. Then he was gone.

Clearing my mind, I pulled my knees to my chest, hugging them against me. I wanted to see if I could hear them. I'd always heard that you could expand your senses by focusing on them. I wanted to try. As I listened, I noticed the forest was quieter than normal. I wondered if it had to do with all the predators running around, scaring the prey.

Taking a deep breath, I let it out and focused on the light breeze. The leaves around me gently twitched. A small branch fell from a canopy a short distance from me. I listened to the forest, waiting to hear something familiar. Then I heard a small voice. It was as if the words came from the end of a long hallway. The words were drowned out and soft but I could understand some of the words.

Stay hidden until she is gone.

I didn't know what to think. Who were they hiding from? Why? I wanted to find them and ask them but it was so strange. Even though I knew what they said, it was as if it were in a different language.

A roar startled me. My eyes popped open as I listened to the commotion that seemed miles away. Then not far to my right another roar erupted. I waited but nothing else happened. Straining my ears, a twig broke to my left. My heart thumped in my ears. Were the people I heard running for their lives? My eyes widened as I slowly turned in the direction of the noise. A shadow slipped into the sun and my breath caught in my throat. It wasn't a person but a panther.

Greg. I would never forget his greenish, yellow eyes.

I froze as he strolled past. I hoped he wouldn't know I was there but then he stopped, mid-stride, raised his nose into the air and his eyes locked on me.

My body shivered from the death stare. I wanted to move, to run but I was frozen like water in a fifty below zero lake. He came forward, lips curled up, showing long white fangs. I wasn't letting him kill me so I made myself move. I crab-crawled backward as he came into the underbrush. When I broke free of the bushes, I gripped a branch when my hand slide across it and came to my full height.

Greg's ears laid back and his tail twitched from side to side. He looked mad and I was the reason. I'd screwed up his plans and he wanted to get even with me, one way or another.

Holding the limb like a baseball bat, I waited for him to get closer. If he did, I would hit him like a home run over center field. He growled, moving to my right. His muscles rippled with each step. The beat of my heart deafened me as he sized me up. I gripped the handle of my stick, anticipating his pounce, shaking from the fear that coursed through my veins.

Instead, he shimmied up the tree. I didn't know what to do as he climbed out on the limb above me. Should I run? Back paddling, I watched his razor claws biting into the bark. The limb swayed under his weight then he jumped.

Claws were all I saw.

The sharp points shined as if each one was a star flashing for me to see before they ripped into my body. My eyes widened at the sight but I refused to fall without a fight. I swung my bat with every ounce of energy I had. The branch struck him on the side of the head, causing my arms to shake from the impact of hitting what felt like a concrete wall. The sound of the branch breaking and a growl shot into the stillness. My forearm came up, blocking his teeth from sinking into my neck.

He slammed into me, knocking me to the ground. His claws dug into my shoulder. I screamed from the searing hot pain that ripped through me. My head bounced against the dirt, as I tried to pull my feet up to keep him off f me. Tears blurred my vision but I kept fighting. I kicked and punched using whatever I could to keep him from ripping my throat out.

In slow motion, his paw rose above me. He extended his razor-sharp claws. The sun highlighted the nails, the large pads on his paw. My heart thumped, rushing the blood to my ears. I couldn't breathe. I couldn't scream. I watched, waiting for him to strike.

From nowhere, a black streak hit Greg, rolling him off of me. The hiss and roar of the cats fighting filled the forest. I tried to move but I couldn't take my eyes from the fight. It was deafening, deadly and I was terrified even more now. My eyes felt like they would pop out of my head because they were opened so wide.

Fear shot through me for Carter. I knew he could fight. If he was there leader, he had to prove himself that way. I was afraid of what Greg would do to win. He was irrational and a panther which made it worse—double crazy.

Yet it didn't take long for Carter to prove why he was their leader.

Randy and Joe came from the forest just in time. They watched as their leader sank his jaws into the rogue panther. Roars filled the forest as Carter sliced Greg's belly, spilling his eternal organs onto the ground. Greg's hollow yellow eyes fell to the ground. I stared at him as they stared back.

A different roar came from behind me. I turned to see Ethan with Sarah at his side. "Sarah," I called through the pain that seemed to magnify with each breath.

She ran to me. Her eyes were wide as they worked across my body. Without a thought, she wadded up my shirt and pressed it into the wound. Despite the pain, I smiled at her. It was so good to see that she was safe and where she belonged.

Through gritted teeth, I said, "I'm sorry I left you."

"It's OK." Her eyes scanned the forest as she tried to figure out what to do.

With each beat of my heart, the pain rose. I broke out into a cold sweat and I couldn't keep from shaking. To keep from screaming, I gritted my teeth and relaxed in the leaves. I fought to keep my eyes open, looking up at the sun's rays that slipped through dark branches and green foliage. *At least I'm where I belong,* I thought.

The world began to spin. Carter lay next to me. The softness of his fur pressed against my skin.

Prying my eyes open, I looked at him. His eyes held more than you would expect to see in an animal. He was afraid and so was I. I didn't want to die. I'd finally found a place that made me feel like I belonged. I didn't have to pretend to be something I wasn't.

"Don't be sad," I whispered.

The world twisted, making my stomach fill empty. I felt as if I were falling, surrounded by darkness. My eyes grew heavier as my breath became shallow until I couldn't hold them open any longer and breathing was too hard. Then everything went dark.

Chapter 23

Lights hovered around me as if I floated in black water. The golden colors drifted about, a hint of a reflection in each one. My body ached. My limbs felt heavy as if they were weighted down with cement blocks. My heart raced. The sound of my blood rushing through my body deafened me.

The colors grew, focusing on an image. I was sucked into a room. A man stood before me. A tall dark haired man, with an affectionate smile and kind blue eyes that appeared to be in his forties, stared at me. I didn't know him but I did...My mind worked. There was something about him that was familiar. I felt like I'd met him before or seen him in passing.

The golden hue faded back to black, swirling lights erupted as before and worked around me. I looked out at a castle—two tall towers nestled in next to a waterfall that fell from the heavens. I couldn't believe my eyes. People—Faeries, popped into my head—walked about. One of them twisted and transformed into a deer before my eyes. My heart picked up to an unhealthy rate.

Again it changed. I stood before a young man. His eyes were the color of oranges. His hair was thick on top and looked as if he spent hours on it. He was cute with his baby face and to straight of a nose. The man raised his hands. Words slipped out of his mouth in a language I didn't know…but I did. My breathing rushed in and out of my slightly opened mouth. In the core of my body, heat erupted. It pulsated until it filled my entire structure. It felt as if I were on fire. I tried to scream. I tried to run but all I could do was look down at my blue dress. Flames that were orange, purple and blue danced around me. I watched as my dress fell to the rock floor and my body was consumed by fire turning into ash.

I sat up with a gasp. My heart thundered in my chest. I couldn't take a deep enough breath, sucking it in so fast. My eyes worked around the room.

I wasn't where I should've been. It was a plain room with a queen bed and a dresser against the wall at the foot of the bed. Two doors were on either side of the cabinet. The one on the right was slightly open while the other was closed. A dark blue curtain hung over the only window at my right, letting light slip in around the edges.

I tried to move. My body ached in places I never knew could hurt. I had a bandage wrapped around my left side, keeping my arm across my chest. My shoulder was packed with a ton of gauze. I stretched. At least I was in a comfortable bed and not in the cot I'd slept in or the dirt of the cave. Anything was better than the cage.

Pulling the blanket up to my face, I inhaled. The scent of home hit me with a hug. The intoxicating smell I didn't ever want to be without filled my nose. Closing my eyes, I thought of Carter. I was lying in his bed. I hid the smile that spread across my face with the cover. *I'm in his room.*

The door on the left wall opened. Becca peeked in at me. Her eyes sparkled when she saw me. Even though I didn't know her that well, I was happy to see her. And the tray of food she was carrying made me even happier.

"You got to be hungry." She smiled as she set the tray down next to me on the bed. There were a hamburger, fries and a piece of chocolate cake. It was perfect. "Mandy filled it for you."

I smiled because Mandy knew me so well.

"Thanks." My mouth salivated over the food; however, my body felt like a dried out piece of clay so I took the bottle of water. I held it for a moment wondering how I was going to open it then Becca took it from me and twisted off the lid.

She handed it back. "How are you feeling?"

"Tired. Sore." I exhaled. "How's Sarah?"

Sitting down, she answered, "She's having a little trouble with Werecats. It's strange, though. She ain't even freaked out about them." She shrugged. "Ethan said she knew him when he pounced on Bob. She ran right to him and hugged him."

I took a few bites of my food. "She's smart. I think she figured it out a while ago."

She narrowed her eyes at me. "When did you figure it out?" she questioned.

"After the party," I admitted, "I heard all the growls and fighting. When I asked Carter, he wouldn't give me a straight answer so I had a feeling there was more to it." I sighed as I let my few bites settle. "But it doesn't sink in until you see someone change."

"You saw Greg change?"

Shaking my head, I said, "No. He was already that way. A cat…Werecat. It was someone else. I didn't hear his name—" I sat up. "There were four. Did you get all of them?" Panic washed over me at the thought he could come back for me.

She tried to get me to relax. "You're fine. It was just Justin. He disappeared. We figured Greg killed him because he wasn't one of the smart ones."

Resting back on the pillow, I added, "He must've been the one diverting you to the Rivals while they took us in the opposite direction." I stuck my fork into the cake. "Who are the Rivals?"

She laughed as she stood. "Carter has a lot to explain but first…" She opened the door. "Your friends want to see you."

Chapter 24

Mandy burst through the door with Sarah. Tony and Rob followed close behind with smiles I was glad to see. It was wonderful to know they were safe. They were the first real family I had. There were many foster kids that I grew up with, ones I tried to protect but I never experienced this before. Feeling this way was strange, foreign to me and I wasn't certain how to act on it.

Mandy and Sarah crawled into the bed with me. Sarah smiled but she kept her eyes down. Mandy, on the other hand, was her typical perky self. It was as if Sarah and I hadn't been taken by psychos. I imagined in Mandy's eyes, we were locked in a room with no electric or running water. *If she only knew*, I thought.

"You look better," Mandy mentioned.

Tony made a gross face from the foot of the bed. "Your bruises are pretty gruesome though." He grinned at Rob as he nudged him with his elbow.

I had a feeling it looked horrific. "Is it awful?" My hand automatically touched my lip then my eye.

"No." Rob smiled. "Think of them as pride wounds."

Glancing at Sarah, I noticed she was back in the shell she was in when we first met. "I'm sorry, Sarah," I told her. "I knew if I kept Troy focused on me and away from you, you'd be safer." I took a breath. "I didn't want to leave you…I didn't know what to do…but I had to do something."

Tears filled her eyes. "You did the right thing. If you hadn't run, we would be god knows where." She took my hand and finally looked up at me. "I don't blame you for anything."

The room became quiet. The sounds from outside the door hummed with the muddled voices of others. I didn't want to consider what might've happened if I hadn't taken a chance. We could've been taken to a different country or worse, killed.

A big smile spread across Mandy's face. "So," she began, "how do you feel about Werecats?"

It surprised me that she knew. I glanced around at each of my friends, expecting them to be freaked out but they weren't.

I shrugged. "I like most of them." *One in particular.*

Tony chimed in, "I think it's cool."

"Only because Becca's one," I said with a hint of laughter.

He couldn't contain his smile as he nodded. "Probably."

"They asked us to join," Rob said.

I looked at him. "Who us? All of us?"

"Yeah," he answered. "If we want to."

Searching each of their faces, I wondered if it was something they wanted. "Are you considering it?" It was a life-changing decision.

"I already said yes," Tony blurted out. "I'm coming back next summer so Carter can change me."

I stared at Tony. *Why*? Then I thought about his home life. He was similar to me but different. At least he knew who his parents were even though they weren't ever home.

"Are you sure it's what you want?" I asked him.

He nodded. "Joining the Army was something I was considering but you know I'm not good with the authority thing. I can't handle someone in my face." He crossed his arms. "Carter sat with me after he heard you were going to be OK. We talked a while…They do things differently…not forcibly. They're family."

Tony spoke like a different person. He seemed so wise, so grown up and knowing it was a family to him, made me want it more than I already did.

"Rob, what about you? You can't change your plans with the Marines can you?"

"Mitch, Carter's brother, runs the same camp filled with Navy and Marines. He said I had a place in Georgia if I wanted it."

I couldn't believe it. My friends had their lives planned out in a few days or hours. Where was I when they decided? *Oh yeah,* I thought, *in a cage. On the run...Dying...*

"I'm going with Rob," Mandy added. "I'm not going to be a Werecat but I will be teaching them. Can you believe they offered me a full ride to any college in Georgia?"

"Really?" Most people in our little town didn't get the chance to go off to college. Some were lucky but others stayed at the local community college. I wasn't saying the degrees at the community college weren't good but only a few could actually pay for it. A few of us had other means...

I was glad they were getting a chance at a life most dreamed of. It made me wonder if I would I get the same choice? Would Carter ask me if I wanted to be part of his family? Did he see me as being an asset to his pride?

I glanced at Sarah. She kept her head down while everyone told me what they wanted. How did she feel about the big secret they kept here? Was she on board?

"What about you, Sarah?" I wondered.

"I'm not sure what I want to do." She sighed. "I don't want to say yes now and in three years change my mind or the opposite." She looked up at me. "Ethan understands. He's giving me all the time I need to think about it."

When she said his name, her cheeks flushed. I'd never seen her as happy as she was when he was with her. Was it possible to fall in love so fast? "So you're going to stay in touch?"

Nodding, she grinned. "Mom will be upset when he visits but he says he will. I don't doubt anything he says."

We all smiled, feeling good that everyone was in this room, happy, safe and looking forward to what was to come. I felt lucky to have survived an attack.

"What about you, Chris. Are you thinking of becoming a shape-shifting panther?" Tony asked.

I thought about everything my friends had said, about my and Carter's talks. I was interested in becoming one of the pride but I still had some questions before I made my final decision. One thing was clear though, I would do it for one reason—family. It was all I wanted and if becoming a panther gave me my dream, I'd seriously think about it.

"I'm thinking about it."

Chapter 25

A pounding erupted on the door. It opened and Carter came in with a smile I had missed. My heart felt as if it leaped out of my chest at the sight of him. I'd always felt something for him but now it felt stronger than before.

"Do you mind if I talk to Christa?"

They each said their goodbyes while Carter stood at the door waiting for them to leave. When they were finished with telling me they would see me later, Rob had to push Mandy out the door.

When Carter shut the door, he stood there for a moment. I hadn't seen him as the tall boy, with a somewhat lanky body, since the day he took me to the waterfall. It felt like an eternity ago. The moment his blue eyes met mine, my breath caught in my throat. An electricity seemed to rise in the atmosphere around us. The hairs on my arms rose and I felt as if I was being pulled toward him. I know he felt the draw because he quickly averted his eyes and then he ran a hand through the top of his blondish hair.

I didn't want him to feel awkward or anything so I tried to take his mind off of it. "Nice room."

Carter walked over and sat next to me, ignoring my comment. He picked up the tray with a soft grin and set it on the floor. "The bed is more comfortable than the cots."

"Yes, it is." I wiggled deeper into the pillows. *And it smells good too.*

He grew silent, uncomfortable even, as his eyes went from everywhere except on me. I could tell something was on his mind. It caused a frown to work across his brow. I hadn't seen this emotion on him before. I hoped it wasn't the brief moment we had.

I took a breath and gently reached out my hand. My fingers twitched just before I rested them on his leg. "What's wrong?" I hoped the comfort of my touch helped him get through what ate at him.

He let out a ragged breath as he leaned over and slid his arm around my waist. "I have to tell you something and I'm afraid you will hate me for it." Even though his face held the worry, his voice was full of pain. It reminded me of the way his eyes looked in the forest when he lay next to me. When I thought I was dying.

Did I die?

"Remember when I told you, you would get a choice. It would be up to you if you wanted to join Army Pride?" I nodded, feeling my throat tighten. "I wanted you to choose to be a member…" His fist in his lap clinched. The knuckles turned white from the force. "You might've considered staying for me."

I wanted to look into his eyes, to see if the words he spoke mirrored the emotion I know he held in his baby blues. I quickly looked back at his hand, at his leg and at my fingers resting on his pants. My fingers dug into his thigh, gripping his jeans. "What are you saying?" Please don't be what I think it is.

He glanced at my shoulder. "Greg scratched you." A sound like a growl came from deep inside. "He nearly ripped your arm off." His jaw clenched. When his eyes met mine, I could read all the uncertainty he had boiling up inside of him and he didn't have to say another word. I knew. I believed I knew when it happened.

My breathing became labored as my eyes darted around the room. He took my hand, gently caressing the top with his thumb. His arm around my waist tightened.

"When you get bitten or scratched by someone like us in our animal form," he paused then continued, "You become one of us."

I sucked in a shaky breath. "I'm a—a…" The word wouldn't leave my mouth. It roared in my head, mocking me. Greg's ugly face said it as if he were proud of what he had done to me. Even though it hurt, I wouldn't let him have the power of making me feel like a victim. I'd been one most of my life, going from family to family. Begging for attention, food or a bed. I wouldn't do it any longer. I was stronger than anyone expected.

So I took a steady breath, relaxing. "I'm a Werecat now?" My voice was calmer than I felt.

The look on his face told me he disliked Greg for what he'd done to me. Carter wanted me to choose my fate. Greg stole that right from me. I believed that was why Carter killed him.

He nodded. "The first few times you change it will be hard, painful but I'll be here and Becca will too. You will never be alone."

I dropped my head, staring at the cover. How would this work? It explained why they never accepted recruits under the age of eighteen. They live out in the middle of nowhere so they can't be seen by anyone. I was a ward of the state. How could I live here? How could I keep this secret from anyone?

"How am I going to do this?" I asked, "I'm in high school."

"I know and you can still go." There was a hint of amusement in his voice. "I did."

I looked at him with a frown. "You did?"

"I was born this way, Christa."

That surprised me. "Really?"

He nodded. "You'll have to come here one time a month so you can shift to let your panther side run. If you don't, the call will drive you crazy." He touched my face. His eyes took in my eye that hurt and to prove it, it throbbed with each beat of my heart.

Stupid Troy, I thought.

"She's a part of you now and you have to let her know she is important too. It will take some time getting used to her inside your head but you can do it." He smiled. "I have no doubt you will be fine."

My entire life I'd been put into categories: an orphan, foster kid, weirdo, trash. Now I'd be one more and I couldn't hold my emotions any longer. After all, I'd kept my cool in the cage for Sarah. I fought back when Troy was after me. I survived a panther attack. I didn't cry through it. I didn't cry most of my life being shuffled place to place. I had to be strong, emotionless but sometimes enough was enough.

Tears dripped down my face. I didn't bale like a blabbering idiot. My brain was on overload, hearing about what I would, have become. I always wanted to be different but not like this. I wanted a family. I wanted parents who cared where I was at night. I didn't want to be something that was a myth.

Carter pulled me to him. I felt like he was afraid I would blame him but I knew it wasn't his fault. He didn't do this to me. Carter killed the one who cursed me. He protected me and I would always be grateful for it.

His arms held me close to him. One hand gently slid along my back in a comforting touch, trying to soothe me. I relaxed against him. My entire body seemed to let loose and I cried. Tears welled in my eyes and streamed down my face as I shook against him. Snot and tears bleed out onto his shirt.

"I'm sorry, Christa."

Baling his tee-shirt into my hand, I tried to pull him closer. I felt safe in that position. With him, I never felt as if I was in danger and I never wanted to let it go.

There was a light tap on the door. "What?" Carter called in a tone louder than when he talked.

From the other side, Becca answered, "Mitch needs you."

He sighed. I sniffled and sat back, rubbing the back of my hand across my face.

"Feel better?" he asked. I nodded even though I didn't. He stroked my hair for a minute then kissed the top of my head.

Great, I thought. The first kiss I get was when I look and felt like garbage.

He walked over to the door. "I'll be back later. How 'bout I bring you…" He smiled. "Ice-cream?"

I couldn't help but smile at him. He had that effect on me. "Chocolate?"

Smiling, he said, "You got it." Then he winked before he left me in his room alone with only the joy of ice-cream for later.

Chapter 26

Becca came in after he'd left, carrying a box of tissues. I supposed no one could miss Carter's snot infested tee-shirt. I huddled back in the covers, pulling them up to my face while I tried not to feel sorry for myself. I was the one who wanted a different life and I got it, even if it wasn't the way I expected.

"Here you go." She set the box down next to me. I instantly pulled one free and wiped my nose. "A lot of info all at once will do that to the strongest person." She sat down. "Maybe you could focus on the benefits."

What could be the plus to this? "Like what?"

"Well," she began, "You don't ever get sick. You have a kickass metabolism, you heal super fast and," she smiled as she added, "You age gracefully."

"Really?"

"We're not immortal. We do die it's just after about hundred and fifty years."

Wow, I thought. I would outlive most of the people I know. If I had a family that would worry about me it would be different but I didn't. It was only me and my friends. They wanted to be this…but could I do it?

After a few heartbeats, I asked, "Do I have to get naked to change?" The image of the boy I'd seen change rushed through my mind. "I don't want to." My eyes widened. "Especially not in front of Carter."

Call me crazy but I didn't think nudity was free speech. Besides, I had enough concerns with my own body image. I didn't need someone else judging me. Mostly, I didn't want a guy to see me in my birthday suit who I'd actually like to kiss someday.

She grinned at me as if she could hear my inner ramble. "You'll get used to it. At first, Helena and I will be with you, to coach you through the change then it'll be up to you."

Helena, I wondered who she was. Was she a Werecat whisperer or something? "Who is she anyway?"

"Mitch's wife." She frowned. "It's Carter's older brother's wife. She's great. They decided to stay when they found out you were clawed."

"Stay? Where were they?"

"Carter called them in." She lowered her voice. "Between us, I think he wasn't confident in his own skills to find you but we all know he's more than capable of being our leader."

I didn't like hearing he felt that way. It was one thing I liked about him—his strength. I'd never met anyone his age before who seemed so wise. Hopefully, he'd never have those doubts again.

"How do you turn new recruits? I mean is it not like this?" I glanced at my shoulder.

"Hardly. We scratch like a briar." She became serious. "We were worried about you. You lost a lot of blood. It was touch and go for a few heartbeats." Then she smiled. "But you're tough and I know you'll breeze through the shifting stage."

Hearing her say shift caused a ball to form in my throat. "When will I have to…shift?"

She thought. "The Dr. wants you to let your arm heal some then you can change. When you turn back, you'll be good as new."

I smiled slightly. "OK."

"Good." She stood up and went to the door. As she turned the knob and pulled it opened, I wanted to call out to her, to thank her but I didn't. I let her walk out and shut the door behind her.

The entire time I talked to Becca I had a pain similar to a toothache in my cheek. It hurt with each movement I made. When I touched it before, I knew it was swollen but now it felt bigger. Carefully, I touched my cheek. The way it felt, by touch, I was surprised I could see out of my eyes. I could imagine what it looked like and the realization made me regret Carter seeing me like this.

I scooted off the bed, so I could go to the bathroom. My feet touched hardwood. It took a moment to stand, allowing my muscles to adjust to my weight. When I was steady, I wobbled to the bathroom because every part of my body hurt.

Pushing the door inward, I flipped on the light that was just inside the door frame. It was an average sized room with a tub shower combo, a single white sink and a commode next to it.

I kept my eyes down as I squared up in front of the sink, ready to look in the mirror at myself. Letting my hand rest on the porcelain top, I gripped the edge. I stared at my dirty legs with scratches, bruises and dried blood on them. My feet were cleaner—a visible line of white where my shoes and ankle socks were. Then I sucked in a breath to look at my reflection in the mirror.

There was a dark line on my lip that rested on a purple bruise. A multitude of colors took up half my face but focused on my eye. Tears blurred my vision as I stared at a girl I didn't recognize. I had met her years ago when a foster mom smacked me around. She never gave the kids enough to eat, so I gave the younger one's half of my portions. When she found out…Let's just say they took me away from her after my few nights in the hospital.

I swore I'd never let someone treat me like that again. My body shook. My knees wobbled from the frustration of being shoved back into that place again. I never wanted to feel lost or weak.

It could've been worse, I thought. *You stopped it.*

Taking a breath, I nodded to myself. I didn't let him do this to me. I even fought back. I was proud, in a way.

I looked down at my clothes. My shirt hung off of me in strips. My heart sank to my toes. The thought of sleeping in Carter's bed caked in gross nasty...*Oh gosh;* I swallowed the lump in my throat. He sat next to me and I'm sure I smelled like garbage.

Turning to the tub, I knew what I wanted to do. I twisted the water on then I began taking my clothes off. Trying was the key word. I pulled and tugged but I couldn't get everything off. I needed help. Turning the water back off, I stood there. *Who? Becca?*

I went to the bedroom door and opened it enough I could see through. Carter and Dean were leaning over a small table with a pile of papers scattered across the surface. I glanced around the room but Becca wasn't inside anywhere.

Carter looked up. "Hi. You need something?"

"Um...Where's Becca?" I blushed and looked down at my toes. "I need her to help me with something."

"I'll get her." Dean hurried out the front door.

Carter smiled as he came over. "Is it something I can do?"

My whole body flushed. "I wanted to take a bath." He slipped into the room, barely touching me as he went by. He walked straight to the bathroom as if he was going to help me. "Would you go get my clothes from the cabin for me?"

"I will." He stopped at the dresser, pulling out a shirt and shorts. "Use these until I can get yours." Then he went into the bathroom and set them down on the sink and opened the cabinet door. "Everything you need is in here."

I leaned against the door. He was pretty amazing. The craziest part, I was standing in his bathroom and I could melt in his gaze. Then I remembered what my face looked like. Without another thought, I threw my hand up to shield him from my face.

"What are you doing?" He stepped forward, taking my hand and lowering it.

"I don't want you looking at me like this. It's ugly."

His finger lifted my chin as he stared down at me. "You are not ugly." The corner of his mouth came up with a crooked grin. "You are beautiful."

My heart banged into my chest as if each beat drew me closer to him. He cupped my face, staring down at me. I felt like I was the only person alive. I wanted him to kiss me. I wanted to know what it was like to have his lips smother me, devour me. My breath caught at the idea.

"Becca's here," she sang from the doorway.

My breath came out in a poof.

A smile slowly stretched across his face before he turned to her. "We can see that."

He gave me one more glance before he walked out of the bathroom and into the bedroom. I didn't want him to go. "Carter," I called as I followed.

He turned to me, holding the doorknob. "Christa?"

Why did my name sound so good coming out of his mouth? I could melt into the floor and be happy for an eternity. "Don't forget the ice-cream."

He gave me the biggest grin I'd seen yet. "Chocolate?"

I nodded. "Please."

"You got it." He walked out and I turned back to the bathroom where Becca stared at me. I instantly wished for a whole to climb into for the look that was written all over my face.

Chapter 27

Even though I felt crazy for how I acted with Carter, and Becca witnessed it, I was glad she was here to help me. She stood in the bedroom, her hands on her hips. Her Army shirt looked fierce with her black shorts. She was a real looker one would say.

"So what do you need?" she asked.

I walked over to the bathroom door and motioned to the tub with a nod. "Will you help me take this off," I pulled at my shirt, "And wash my hair?" When I looked at it in the mirror, there were bits of twigs and leaves buried inside the nest of knots. It was totally gross.

I turned the water back on and turned to Becca. She eyed my shirt. "It's ruined?"

"I'd say so." It was a good thing I wore a sports bra because otherwise, I'd been bare.

She opened a drawer on the cabinet and pulled out a pair of scissors then she started cutting. After all my dirty clothes hit the floor, I climbed in. It was hard trying not to get my bandages wet buy when it came down to washing my hair, Becca was a champ. She used a cup to wet my mane, soaped it up and rinsed it.

She sat on the commode while I relaxed in the water. "Now that I'm one of the Pride what would I do here?"

"Nothing now." She smiled. "But Carter wants you to be his Alpha female."

I didn't know the rule of Werecats but that didn't seem right to me. "Doesn't that bother you? I mean you've been a Panther longer than me."

"No way." She laughed. "Carter's more of a brother to me."

"So it doesn't go with seniority?"

She shook her head. "It's about the connection you have with the other. When your cat finds its mate then you will only want to be with that person. And since Carter is an Alpha his mate will be one also."

Could I be an Alpha? The more I thought about it, I'd like to but what does Carter really think of me? He doesn't know me. I haven't told him about my family or lack of one. Would he walk away because I didn't have what he does?

"What would I have to do if I chose it?"

"You would be the co-leader. But you can't officially join until you're eighteen."

As I swirled the washrag in the water, I wondered about the Werecats. Where did they come from? Why were they fighting with a group called Rivals? It seemed like I was asking more questions then I was having answered.

"I haven't had a chance to ask Carter so maybe you can tell me who the Rivals are?"

"When I joined, I was told they are an enemy from way back like the Hatfield's and McCoy's. It started one day, no one knows why for sure, they just don't like Carter's family."

"It started with Carter's family?"

"The war? Yeah but Carter's family tree isn't huge. There aren't many like them."

We talked so much about Carter, the Rivals and what it meant if I stayed here as an Alpha. It was nice talking about the future as if I had some potential with them. I never had that advantage. I was lucky to spend a year with one family. Having someone covet me, for me to be with them, wanting me to be here made me feel like I'd never felt before.

After my bath, Becca helped me into Carter's clothes, he loaned me, then I said my goodbyes and crawled into the bed with clean sheets Becca and I changed. Now, I was ready for my ice-cream date with Carter. Well, he might not have said that was what it was but I was going to call it that.

Chapter 28

I got tired of lying in the bed so I stood next to the window. Peeking through the side of the curtain, I watched as my friends and other members of the group went on about their day. The sun shined down on them making me wish I was with them, enjoying the time we'd spent together.

The door opened behind me. I turned to see Carter walk in with my duffle bag over one shoulder and a pint of ice-cream in his hand. The smile on my face instantly appeared. He just had that effect on me.

He eyed me as he pushed the door closed with his foot. "That shirt looks better on you than it ever did on me." He smiled from his comment.

I glanced down at the gray tee with faded blue writing. I doubted that. So I rolled my eyes to make sure he understood how crazy that sounded. "Sure," I mumbled. He looked good in everything I saw him in.

"You look like you're feeling better."

"I do," I pointed to my face," until I look in the mirror."

"You have a good reason to look that way, besides it'll go away in a few days." He set the bag down next to the dresser.

"I fought a guy who outweighed me by at least fifty pounds."

He sat on the bed, took my hand and pulled me down next to him. "You gave as much as you got."

The look on his face was strange. It was as if he were proud of me. Did I impress him by fighting back?

He held the ice-cream up. "What do ya say we get comfortable and enjoy our chocolate ice-cream?"

We lend against the headboard with our legs stretched out. He handed me a spoon and opened the lid. Then he held it out so I could take the first bite and I did. I wasn't passing up ice-cream for any reason.

I quickly spooned out a dollop and shoved it into my mouth. The sweet chocolaty goodness coated my tongue. It sat there for a moment, to melt, and then I swallowed. It was delicious.

"So, where did you sleep since I took over your room?"

"On the couch."

I didn't like that he put me in here. This was his room and he shouldn't show me any special attention. I didn't deserve it. "You should've put me in my bunk."

"I promised you I would take care of you. When Greg hurt you…" He took a breath as if the words were too much to say. "I broke that promise. I shouldn't have left you there alone."

Are you blaming yourself? It wasn't his fault. I slipped my arm through his and leaned against him. "It wasn't your fault. I wanted to go. Me. If you hadn't let me, I would've come on my own."

He cracked a grin as he stared at me. "Yeah, I believe you would've."

"You bet your butt I would have." I smiled feeling better than I had in a long time.

When the ice-cream was gone, we sat like that, staring at the wall with the dresser and the door to a closet and a bathroom. I could stay like that forever, listening to the air entering and leaving his lungs and feeling the warmth of his skin on my arm. It was nice.

"I was wondering," he began, "how'd you know it was me on the trail? It could've been any one of us."

As I thought how to answer it, I felt silly. Would he understand? "Your eyes. They don't change and you smell the same."

He made a funny face and lifted his arm to smell himself. "Do I stink?"

"No." I shook my head. "When we were dancing, you smelled like the woods. Not the wet wood scent but a good fresh stream one." I swallowed because my face felt as if it were going to burst into flames. "I smelled it on the trail but when I faced you, I knew it was you."

"I heard you running," his voice was low. "I was doing my patrol along the creek, trying to find any sign. I just kept walking back and forth, waiting. It was like I was meant to be in that spot."

I looked up at him. With each word he spoke, I felt as if he read my heart. It was as if I were meant to be here in this place at this moment. Maybe it was fate. Our destiny—to be together here in this time and space.

"I ran. I got there in time to see you slug him." He smiled. "I'd never been as happy to see someone before in my entire life."

I felt that joy as I stared into his eyes of blue. My heart seemed to skip every other beat. How was it possible that each moment I spent with him I fell just a little bit more. It wasn't normal to have feelings so fast.

"I couldn't believe I made it. You startled him, keeping him from dragging me to whatever dump they had planned for us next." I took a breath. "I kept telling myself to find you that everything would be fine as long as I did." I glanced at my toes. "You found me instead."

He took my hand, sliding his fingers between mine. His eyes were focused on it as if it held a question he needed to ask. "Ethan talked to Sarah about what had happened to yons. I didn't pry." He sighed. "Would you tell me? Did they…" His breathing picked up.

Oh, I thought. "They kept us in a cage. They didn't bother us, not really." I kept the part about peeing in a can to myself. Even if Sarah told Ethan and he told Carter, I didn't care. I just didn't want to relive the humiliation.

I ran my tongue across my teeth. *Gross*. It felt like I had an inch of goo on my teeth. I got up and went to my duffle bag. As I rummaged around, I could feel Carter's eyes on me.

"Did I forget something?"

"I was looking for my toothbrush."

He walked over and unzipped a side pocket and handed me my pink toothbrush and the toothpaste. He actually looked cute holding it out to me. I smiled and took them then went to brush my teeth.

When I was finished, he was sitting at the foot of the bed, watching as I exited the bathroom. I paused for a moment wondering why he was staring at me. He did that a lot, it seemed.

"Are you ready?" he asked.

I was confused. "For what?"

"Mitch and Helena want to meet you."

I stared at him with my mouth slightly a jar. My breath stuck in my throat. My racing heart had blood rushing through my body so fast, I was deafened by it.

Oh no, I thought. *What if they don't like me?*

Chapter 29

"Are you serious?"

He nodded.

"I don't think I should be meeting someone for the first time looking like this." I sulked as I frowned at myself. "Especially not your family."

He smiled and stepped to me. "You look great."

Was he blind? "I look like I just crawled out of bed."

A mischievous expression crawled across his face. "You did." He glanced at the bed then at me. "But you still look good."

I quickly looked at my toes because each time he said something that embarrassed me, my entire body erupted into flames. "Shut up."

Carter held his hand out for me to take. "Come on."

I took a breath as I accepted his hand, wondering if I would ever win a fight with him. "Do I need shoes?" He glanced at my feet so I wiggled my toes.

He smiled. "Probably would be a good idea."

He helped me slip on my extra shoes after I threw the others in the garbage. They weren't new, to begin with, but I never wanted to be reminded of the time I wore them for days and ran for my life.

Carter led me out into the main room. There were a small kitchen, a living room and two more doors in the back.

"Who stays with you?" I glanced at the doors behind the kitchenette.

"Dean and Becca." He pointed to the door they stayed in.

"It's nice." It was a beautiful quaint cabin.

Opening the door, he motioned me out into the evening sun. I walked down the few steps and looked around at the facility. He walked up next to me and slipped his arm around me. I leaned into him as we walked toward the mess hall and stopped at the last cabin on the left. At the top of the steps, Carter knocked on the wooden door.

A tall woman with vibrant green eyes, shoulder length blonde hair and a round face opened the door. "Carter." She smiled. "Come in." she stepped to the side so we could enter. "Christa, it's good to see you up and moving."

I smiled at her. "Thank you." There was an essence to her. I instantly understood why the others automatically liked her. I just walked into the room with her and I felt as if she were my best friend.

"Mitch," she called to the room next to the living room. "Carter and Christa are here."

Carter introduced me, "Christa this is Helena."

I said, "It's nice to meet you."

She took my hand. "I'll settle for your hand but soon as you're better, I get a hug."

"She's a hugger," Carter teased.

"Yes, I am." She lifted her chin with pride.

The cabin was more or less an exact replica of Carter's. The colors were a little softer but the same layout and the same furniture.

Mitch came out of the bedroom and I instantly saw the resemblance. "Christa." He extended his hand and I took it for a quick shake.

"Hello." Mitch was older than Carter by maybe five years. His build was wider and his arms were more muscular. The one thing they had in common was their blue eyes. I'd never seen two siblings with an exact eye color. The blue was so vibrant and breathtaking.

We sat on the couch. Carter held my hand while I stared at my knees. I could feel them staring at me. I wasn't very comfortable being the center of attention.

"Carter has told you what has happened?" Mitch broke the silence.

I nodded as I glanced up at them. Mitch sat in an armchair while Helena sat on the arm at his right.

"The change the first time will be..." he thought. "Painful."

My eyes widened. *Nobody told me that.*

"I'm not going to lie to you."

Helena interrupted. "Becca and I will coach you through the transformation." Her voice hummed with confidence. "Carter will help you while you are in cat form."

I remembered the way the others acted when they were in their panther forms. It was as if they could talk to one another. "How will we communicate?"

"You'll be able to hear his voice as if he is talking to you."

I frowned. "In my head?"

Helena added. "Only what you think toward him or another cat, nothing else."

"How is that possible?"

"Carter is the Alpha. Each of his pride will be able to hear him and he will hear them."

I nodded as I swallowed. What else would they say?

Carter sat there letting me listen as Mitch and Helena told me what to do, how to act and what to expect during the shift. I was glad Carter held my hand the whole time because I would've probably run out of the door if he wasn't holding me in place. My heart thumped harder with each word they spoke.

"The cat instincts will want to take control when you shift. The need for blood will be strong the first few times so let her eat so she will know you won't hold her back, give her boundaries though," Mitch told me.

My stomach felt empty. "I have to hunt?" I didn't hurt animals. I didn't kill a mouse.

"Anything but human," Mitch joked.

"We want you to control the shifting before you go home. We don't want you getting mad and shifting in public, attacking someone," Helena added.

Home, I thought. I keep being reminded of the talk I needed to have with Carter. I couldn't fall for him. What if he finds out about my crazy life then leaves? No matter what happened with Carter and me, I had to embrace who I was. I wouldn't sit around and dread the day I'd shift for the first time. I had to do it. It was me, now whether I liked it or not.

"I'm ready to do it."

"It's too soon." Carter shook his head. "You're too weak."

"I feel better. I'm ready to try."

"I don't think it's a good idea."

"We will do it in the morning," I told him.

He didn't like me being demanding but I glanced at Helena. She smiled at Mitch and he glared at Carter. I couldn't help the smile that spread across my face because I'd won my first argument with him. It felt good.

"Fine," Carter said as he stood. "Let's get you to bed."

I stood with him and walked over to the door. Helena pushed Mitch and mumbled something that made him laugh lightly.

"Um…where are you sleeping, Carter?" Helena asked.

He smiled at her. "On the couch, Mom. The same place I did last night."

"You better—" She looked at Mitch for some help.

So he added, "You're young, don't let hormones get the best of you."

Carter frowned. "Seriously? You're four years older than me."

Mitch shrugged. "Just saying."

"You know me better than that."

"I do know you and that's why I'm saying it."

Carter punched him playfully in the arm but his voice told of the frustration he felt, "I'm not a horndog, Mitch."

Mitch became serious. "I know how you feel."

I wanted to crawl into a hole. I didn't need to hear them talk about things I didn't and wouldn't be doing anytime soon. So I pushed the door opened and walked out into the setting sun.

I stood in the warmth of the last few rays of the sun. Closing my eyes, I let my head fall back, absorbing the comfort. Then I inhaled the aromas of nature. It was nice to feel like me. Having the sun on my skin and the breeze slip through my hair reminded me of running. The motion was the one thing that I took with me everywhere I went. It never changed.

The door behind me opened causing me to glance over my shoulder at who exited. Carter laughed lightly as he came down the steps. He inhaled when he stopped at my side.

"He jokes around way too much."

That was him joking? I would hate to find out what he would say if he was serious. I'd been around sex talk for as long as I could remember. It didn't bother me. Well, not until Mitch made me feel as if I were in the spotlight.

Carter had said he believed we had a connection. I knew we did. It felt like my soul was being pulled to him. The age difference did make me worry. I was fifteen. He was eighteen. Most people would think it was wrong.

His fingers slide between mine before he squeezed my hand, bringing me out of my mental debate. "What are you thinking about?"

I wasn't going to bare my soul to him, not yet. I wanted to be sure we were on the same page. "Everything," I told him. "I'm scared." It wasn't a lie.

Carter pulled me into a hug. His arms wrapped around me. I stared up at him while he gazed down at me. One hand came up and pushed the hair back from my face.

In the most caring voice I'd ever heard, "Don't be scared. I'll be with you."

Feeling as safe as I did, scared me. I was starting too depended on him for that safety. It was something I didn't do. I never depended on anyone, for anything. "It's funny; I'm not ever afraid when I'm with you."

His eyes searched my face. "I'll be here always."

My body felt strange. It was as if the blood rushed through it with an unnatural force making me light headed, dizzy even. I laid my head against his chest and inhaled. Why did I love the smell of the forest so much? Why did the smell of trees and earth make me feel at home?

He squeezed me tighter. I felt as if he had so many things running through his mind like I did. Did he enjoy our embrace as much as I do? Did he feel as if he were falling each time he looked into my eyes? I felt that way. I experienced so much more than words could describe. I wanted to know if he thought he loved me because I knew I loved him. I couldn't deny my feelings any longer.

"I'm yours, Christa," he whispered against my head.

I froze there for a moment. Did he just say what I was thinking? Did he read my mind? I didn't care because it was what I wanted to hear.

Chapter 30

"Come on." He led me to his cabin, opening the door for me. Becca and Dean were sitting on the couch watching something with guns blaring out.

"How was the visit?" Becca asked.

Carter laughed. "Good, other than my brother being an idiot."

"It's not only your brother," Dean smirked.

Carter sighed. "Christa is going to shift in the morning."

Becca sat forward. "Are you sure that's a good idea?"

"It's what she wants—"

"Don't talk about me as if I'm not here," I interrupted him. "Besides, Mitch agreed with me."

Dean asked Carter, "You don't?"

"No. I think she, you, should wait."

"I'm not," I told him.

"And I accept that."

Becca smiled. "Aren't you sweet?"

I smiled at Becca. *Yes, he is.*

"Turn the TV down, she's going to bed." He opened the bedroom door for me.

I walked in and sat on the edge of the bed, watching him come closer. "I feel bad for taking your room."

"I want you to have it."

"I don't mind going back to my bunk."

He frowned as he came to stand directly in front of me. His hands were on his hips but then he sat next to me in one swift motion. "I want you to stay."

I sighed. "So I've traded a cage for four walls." It came out worse than I meant it to sound.

My words seemed to bother him. "Is that what you think I'm doing?" He stood and took a few steps, frustration on his face. "I'm not keeping you against your will. If you want to go back to your cot then I'll gladly carry your bag for you."

I stood, took a deep breath and walked up to him. I cautiously took his hand. I wasn't afraid to touch him I just wanted to make sure he didn't mind. The roughness of the pads of his fingers was nice. I rubbed my thumb along the meaty flesh of his palm. I didn't want him to feel as if he were treating me the way Greg did and I got that feeling. Carter wasn't that guy. He could never be him. "I want to stay."

My heart raced as his hands came up and cupped my face. He leaned down and pressed his lips to mine. He took me by surprise but it was a good one. The kiss was soft, innocent but it made me feel as if I were on top of the world.

When he stopped, I could barely open my eyes. *Wow*, I thought. My breath was so shallow, I was afraid of suffocating. But it would be worth it.

With that amazing kiss, I realized I had to tell him. I had to spill my secrets to him so he would know who I truly was.

"Can we sit down and talk for a minute?"

He looked at me, confusion slipped across his eyes for a split second. "Sure."

We sat on the bed. He waited patiently as I tried to pull together the words to tell him what I needed to say. I didn't know if he would be like the hundreds of other boys who called me trailer trash because I had no clue who my parents were. *I'm not that girl.*

I took a breath and faced him. His blue eyes took in my face and I diverted my eyes so he wouldn't read my expression—my terrified face.

He frowned. "Uh oh, this ain't good."

"No, it's nothing bad…" I hoped it wasn't for him.

"OK."

"The night at the falls, you told me about your family. I never mentioned mine."

He took my hand as he waited for me to continue.

"I'm not like most girls you've met. See I don't really have a family."

Carter frowned. "You don't have a mom or dad?"

I shook my head. "I have foster parents."

He thought and then asked, "You don't know who your parents are?"

"I was found abandon when I was a baby."

He looked at me and squeezed my hand between both of his. "I'm sorry."

"It's OK. I just thought you should know…I'm different." I thought about how to elaborate. "Not all the families I stayed with were…good."

"Christa."

I looked up into his vibrant blue eyes. My heart thumped in my throat.

"Your being different is one reason I like you so much. You are filled with this determination, drive that I've never seen in another girl before." He took a breath before he added, "If you ever want to talk about your past, I'll listen. I'll even help you find out what happened to them if you want."

I laughed. "I've tried." I shook my head. "There's no record anywhere."

"How about when you're ready to try again, I'll help you," he grinned this stunning smile that made my stomach do a little wiggle, "because I got some connections."

I smiled back as I looked down at his hand holding mine. He sure did have some good ones. "OK." I was so happy he didn't push me away and spit in my face. It's not something I want to live through, again.

He nodded toward the head of the bed. "Bed," he ordered with a smile.

I nodded as I stood so I could brush my teeth and take my shoes off.

He stepped forward and kissed me again before he whispered, "Goodnight, Christa."

"'Night," I said, breathlessly.

He walked out the door and smiled as he closed it behind him. I fell back on the bed with a sigh because I was ready to go to sleep and dream about him. Maybe I would even dream about a future with him.

Chapter 31

I dreamed about the dark haired man again last night. I was little, crying. He picked me up and sat me on his knee. His mouth opened and closed as he spoke to me but I couldn't hear the words. I only felt warmth. His presence made me feel safe. The reason I cried melted away with him holding me.

While he coaxed me from my tears, he held his hand out to me. In his palm, tiny sparkles appeared, growing into a shape of a flower. I smiled at the daisy as I stared at it. I retrieved the bloom from his hand and hugged him. As I breathed in a smell of tobacco, I closed my eyes.

When I opened them, I stared at Carter's bedroom door. A light flickered along the bottom as if the TV was on in the living room. Sighing, I rolled onto my back. My eyes drifted across the ceiling. Why was I having dreams about this man? All of my dreams before were of normal teenage things—boys, movies and crazy things.

I pushed myself up. My arm didn't hurt like it did the day before. It was just tight because I hadn't used it. Sliding off the bed, I went to the bathroom. After I turned the light on, I started removing the bandage. It took a moment to pull off the last gaze. It wasn't because it hurt; it was because I was afraid to see what was under it.

I took a deep breath and treated it like a band-aid. In one swift jerk, I stared at my new scar. It was three, no four, lines that came across my shoulder and arm. When Greg attacked me, I didn't realize how close he came to my neck. Two nails left a pink line about the size of a pencil all the way across my chest, stopping an inch before my sternum. I sighed as I gazed at myself in the mirror.

You were lucky, I told myself.

After one more moan, I went ahead and dressed for the day, even though I wouldn't be wearing clothes. My stomach did a little flip-flop thinking about it. I brushed my teeth and pulled my hair up into a messy ponytail. Then I slipped on my shoes.

As I stood in the bedroom, staring at the door, my stomach growled. I touched it with my hand as I looked at the clock, 4:00 am. It was dark out and still a good hour before everyone got up. I looked at the door again. The light underneath told me someone was up so I opened the door.

My eyes floated around the dark room. The light from the TV highlighted the mostly empty room. Becca sat on the couch with a pillow and blanket folded on the end.

"Hey," she said as she turned to me.

"Morning."

"Sleep well?"

I nodded as I stepped out into the main room. As I made my way to the couch, I asked, "Where's Carter?"

"Shower." She pointed over her shoulder. "He said for me to get you some food."

"Good." I laughed. "'Cause I'm hungry."

She smiled. "You will always be."

We walked out the door and into the dark. Dawn was approaching. You could tell by the way the air felt. Even though it wasn't time for the sun to rise, the air around you was filled with a calmness. I loved to run at this time because it was you and the world, coming alive at the same time.

I picked a little of everything in the mess hall. I was sure I looked like a pig but I didn't care. I wanted it.

Carter came in after my second helping of waffles and bacon. I smiled at him as he walked up in his jeans and a blue tee-shirt. He was gorgeous.

I drank my orange juice and said, "I can't believe I actually ate all of that."

"You'll eat twice that afterward," he said munching on some bacon.

"Did you have weird dreams when you were first turned," I asked Becca.

She frowned. "No, not really."

Carter stared at me. "Did you?"

Should I even consider them? I frowned at my plate. They were odd but something about them made me think I knew who he was. How was that possible? I wondered. I remembered the boy shifting into a panther. How was any of this possible?

"Yeah. Both times I woke up later, I'd dreamed about this man…"

"Uh oh, Carter," Becca teased. "She's dreaming about another."

"No, it wasn't like that." My face felt hot.

"What was it?" He wondered.

"Last night, I dreamed about him," I remembered his smile. "He held me like I was his daughter."

"Maybe he was," Carter added.

I looked at him. "I doubt it."

"Why?" Becca asked.

I glanced around to see if anyone was close. I wasn't for sure if I wanted them to know what else he did in my dream. Yeah, they were shape-shifters but did they believe in witchy magic?

"Do you believe in magic?"

Becca laughed but Carter stared at me with curious eyes. His bacon slowed its ascent to his mouth. He did. He didn't have to say it because it was written all over his face.

"Why did I dream about it?' My question was directed at him and he knew it.

Carter turned to Becca. "Would you give Christa and me a moment? Go see if Helena is ready. We'll meet you at the cabin."

Becca glanced at me then to him. "Sure."

When she was gone, he focused on me. "My ancestors are from a place with magic." He took a breath. "Only my immediate family knows of the things that are taught as myth in this world."

"Does it still exist?"

He nodded. "I've never been but Dad has talked about it before."

My heart seemed to pick up from the news. "Where is it?"

He shook his head. "I'm not sure. You're only able to enter through a portal and we were never told where it was."

I stared at him. He knew more. "Carter, why did I dream about a man who can conjure magic?" I needed him to be honest with me.

"Grandpa talked about where he came from. He called it a magical place with humans that were more. There were other creatures like us but different…" He took a breath. "We swore we wouldn't tell another about it. I shouldn't be telling you."

"Please." I took his hand from the table. "There was something about him that was familiar."

"All I know, it exists. I don't know where or when but magic is real and if you're a part of it, it calls to you."

My eyes widened as I sucked in the biggest breath of my life. "I'm connected to that world?"

He nodded. "Dreams are a way to guide you." He squeezed my hand. "I will help you figure it out."

I nodded, wanting to cry. "Thank you."

"Sure." He stood and pulled me with him. He kissed my lips gently. "Let's meet up with Mitch and Helena."

I nodded as I followed him to the door. "Is it possible my parents are from that world?" I didn't realize my question came out of my mouth until Carter turned to me.

"There is a reason I'm connected to you, Christa. We generally aren't pulled to mortals because of our world, the secrets we have to keep." He stared down at me. "I believe they are."

In a way, I was relieved that he said that. It gave me some hope that I would find them one day.

As we headed out the door, the sun broke the horizon. I realized my fate was planned from the beginning. Like my entire existence, I was a puppet for the world; however, when I shifted into the cat that I would share a soul with, I would take back my life.

Chapter 32

They were waiting for us when we walked into the cabin. The air seemed thick with uneasiness and it made me worry. What was I getting into?

Mitch and Carter took control. They told each of us what to do, when, where and then Carter spoke directly to me. He hugged me. I inhaled his scent while he told me I would be fine. That this was the beginning of a new life for me.

I agreed it was and followed Helena and Becca into his bedroom.

Standing next to the bed, I took a million breaths trying to steady my racing heart. Becca stood next to me while Helena sat on the side of the bed. *I can do this*, I told myself over and over again.

"You're going to be fine, Chris," Becca said, "We'll take care of you."

I was actually excited about being a strong, powerful panther. Being her, I would never be afraid of anything ever again. "It's the being naked I'm a little weird about."

"I was modest," Helena said, "the first time I shifted in front of the pride, I was so nervous."

Becca said, "It's not sexual. It's a necessity. If you change with your clothes on, you could die trying to get them off or get caught."

I took a deep breath and began stripping. When I stood in the bedroom in my birthday suit, I asked, "What do I do now?"

"For the first time," Helena suggested, "lay on your side."

"Don't hold your breath." Becca knelt next to me. "Breathe and try to relax."

"Focus on the instincts that are coming forward from the back of your mind." Helena whispered, "There's a part of you that longs to run, to be free and embrace it."

There was already a part of me that wanted to run. I was free when I stepped into the forest. By being a Werecat, would I feel the same about the woods?

Yet I wondered if it could be as simple as she said.

I closed my eyes and relaxed into the cold hardwood floor. I let my mind roam. From the shadows, a cat came forward. When I thought of running, she ran. I saw her body move, the muscles beneath her soft coat. She was stunning and lethal.

The panther's face came to me. She was black like the others I'd saw but in the sun, she had a purple inlay. Her eyes were dark with flakes of gold around the pupil. She was beautiful. I called to her. She stepped forward causing my skin to tingle. With each step she took toward me, her existence grew on my human form.

"Imagine your body becoming the panther. Slip on your catsuit, starting with the paws," Becca said.

My fingers drew in and expanded. My skin moved as if insects crawled beneath the top layer. Nails grew. In seconds, my human feet and hands had disappeared and in their place was hairless cat paws.

"Good, Chris. Now pull the suit up your legs and arms to your neck." Helena exhaled lightly.

I welcomed the panther. My limbs twisted and popped. I groaned from the pain. The sounds of bones popping and reforming filled my ears. My stomach ached like I had the stomach flu. Gritting my teeth, I tried not to scream; however, the pain that jolted my body was unlike anything I had ever felt. When my body took its new form the pain moved up to the next place to shift. My jaw popped, ripping a scream from my gut.

"This is the hardest part but don't fight it."

My muzzle extended as my nose flattened with the movements. A sharp pain shot down my spine, causing me to wince from the surprise. I thought my jaw hurt when it shifted but this was worse. It felt as if my body turned inside out. My bones were pulled from their joints and moved to new positions.

"Don't fight it," Becca warned. "You're almost there."

I panted. *I can do this*. I stared my panther in the face. When I pulled her to me, it became easier. My new shape slid into place like a puzzle piece fitting into another. My tailbone extended and lengthened into a long thick tail. I squeezed my eyes shut, waiting for it to be over. Then my skin tingled and itched and all of a sudden black fur erupted along my skin.

I lay on the hardwood floor, feeling my muscles contract. I was afraid to move. The air ruffled my fur. I opened my eyes. Everything was different. I saw the world in different colors. I always thought cats could only see shades of gray but I saw the world as I always did. Well, except that my peripheral vision is wider. My ears picked up sounds I'd never noticed before. The best part, the room smelled like Carter.

"Good job," Helena said as she stood.

I rose to my paws. My tail whipped around and nearly smacked Helena in the face. She laughed but I didn't care. There was an energy in me I'd never felt before. I wanted to run, to sprint through the forest. Being the panther felt natural to me. I was her and she was me. It was the most amazing feeling in the world. I only hoped the other Panther's liked me. Would Carter's Panther like me as much as he does? I stared at the door ready to find out if I can live in this world.

Chapter 33

"You ready?" Becca held the doorknob.

I tried to tell her, yes but a weird sound came out instead. They laughed.

"Don't try talking with your mouth. Think it." She pointed to her head. "Carter will do the same with you."

Helena added, "Listen to him."

Becca opened the door. Carter sat on the other side in his cat form. Staring into his blue eyes, I strolled up to him. He rubbed his face against mine. My body felt light and tingly, making me purr. They laughed at me again and I cowered from the realization of my affection for him was broadcasted to the room.

Don't worry about them, Carter's voice came out clear in my mind as if he stood before me. *Focus on me.*

All I could do was stare at him.

Mitch walked up to the door that led outside. "Ready to run?"

I looked at the exit. I wanted to scream yes but I didn't want to sound stupid so I just walked up to it hoping he got the hint.

Mitch opened the door. "Don't stay out too long and watch the border."

Yes, Dad, Carter thought.

Mitch mumbled, "Smartass."

I dove out the door, leaped over the porch and hit the ground with my paws sinking into the soft dirt. The muscles jerked up the front of my legs and into my back. When all my muscles caught up, my hind legs pushed me forward, after Carter. My heart thumped against my ribcage as I ran. The forest called to me. I felt at home surrounded by the thick vegetation. Even before I was a Panther I was one with the wild but this was a different feeling.

Every sound seemed clearer as we cut through the underbrush and dashed under low-hanging limbs. Yet the thing that was more amazing was the smell. It was like a sensory overload of things you didn't know existed. Each one made your mouth water even though you didn't know what it was.

Carter led me down a trail in the opposite direction of the cross-country course we'd run on in the mornings. He stayed next to me, in synchronized steps. I kept bumping into him like a newborn animal learning to walk. He chuckled when I did.

Follow me. He pushed into high gear, tearing across the forest floor through briars and over tree limbs.

Before I knew it, my instincts took hold. They launched me after him and before I knew it, I was on his side so I pushed harder to get out in front.

I dug down in the pit of my stomach, pushing my legs faster. The muscles responded. Inch by inch, I moved in front of him then I exploded past. My lips pulled back in a smile. To the animals in the forest, it probably looked menacing. It didn't matter, it was the happiest I'd been in a long time.

Up ahead, a fallen tree was lying against another forming an incline. I ran up the trunk and lay at the top, looking out at the forest. Carter came up behind me and lay half on and off my hindquarters.

You're a natural.

I smiled because being the panther was the most natural thing in the world to me.

Carter looked out at the forest. His eyes narrowed slightly.

What is it? I asked.

The Rivals' border.

I looked out where he was staring. The trees were painted with a thick lime green line, so anyone who neared the border knew.

A stick broke. Carter stood and so did I. On the other side of the line, a panther walked into the clearing and a few feet behind the cat, two more appeared. I swallowed the knot rising in my throat.

Hello, Rollins.

I looked at Carter. I heard the voice in my head. *Was I supposed to?*

We didn't Cross. Carter slowly made his way down the tree and I followed, making sure to not turn my back on them. *Why are you here?* Carter asked him.

The new Panther took a step closer. *I smell something I hadn't witnessed in years.*

Carter glanced at me and then his voice sank into my head, *Christa, go back.*

I glanced at the others. What was he talking about? Did they hear what Carter said? I didn't want to die in a fight so I listened. I started back to the cabin making sure I kept Carter in my sight as I retreated.

Behind me, a roar shook the trees. The hair on my back rose and I stopped. *Carter?* A second roar followed by a few more. My heart hammered as my eyes searched for any movements. *Carter*, I called to him.

I stood still looking in the direction I came from. Then an awful racket broke the calmness of the forest. Fighting like when I lay on the ground, bleeding to death, filled the wood. *Carter? No*, I thought.

I dashed back toward him. There was no way I would leave him behind with an army of Panthers trying to hurt him. Faster I ran until he came into view. He was tangled in a ball of teeth, nails and fur.

The rival was on Carter's side but the others were on their own. I narrowed my eyes at the panther hurting Carter. I roared as loud as I could, startling them both and attacked.

I ripped, bit and tore into the one who tried to hurt Carter. It only took a second and he hissed and slinked back across his line. I watched his orange eyes, my breath coming in and out in huffs.

Christa. I looked at Carter. *I told you to go.*

When I saw he was OK, I huffed and walked past him toward the cabin.

Christa.

Stopping, I faced him. *Don't ever do that again,* I told him. *I'm not a helpless little girl.*

He laughed. *I know you're not.*

Then why?

Let's shift back then we can talk about it.

I walked next to Carter all the way back to the cabin. I thought about what he needed to say but I worried more about what the Rival said. A new smell…Was it me? All I knew, I was about to find out.

Chapter 34

It took about two seconds to shift back to normal. I felt amazing when I did. My bruises, scars—most, were gone. Everyone told me how proud they were of me and how well I did. When they left, Carter sat down at the little table in the kitchen and pulled the chair out next to him so I could sit in it.

Taking a deep breath, I sat down ready to hear what he had to say.

"I didn't want you near him, Christa."

I frowned. "He could've hurt you."

"He's too old."

"He didn't look old."

Carter sighed. "He and Grandpa came from the same place…"

Then it hit me. He was talking about me. "The dream I had?"

Carter nodded. "Magic is reaching out to you but we have to be careful. There are some bad people who will use that against you."

I took a breath and leaned forward, taking his hand. "Why is magic reaching out to me now?"

He stared at me. His eyes worked across my face. "I don't know but I think we need to talk to Grandpa. I trust him with this."

It felt good, in a way, to know I didn't come from this world I'd grown up in. I sighed internally. This world was as cruel as it was beautiful. It was nice knowing I had him to help me figure out where I belonged.

I leaned forward and kissed him. It was the first time we really kissed. The whole parted lips and tongues. It was amazing, strange even because I felt it in my toes.

"Carter?" He looked into my eyes. His beautiful blue ocean colored pools. "How about some ice-cream?"

He smiled big, showing most of his white teeth. "Chocolate?"

I nodded as he stood up and went to the freezer for a pint. I leaned back in my chair and thought of the man in the woods. The man from my dreams and of this world Carter told me about. There were so many things that I needed to figure out but one thing was settled. I came to this camp looking for a family, the military to be my home and found one with Carter and his Army Pride.

About the Author

Tonya Coffey lives in Stearns, Kentucky with her husband and two teen sons. Together, they inspire her to push her boundaries in whatever she faces. If she isn't reading a fantasy novel with lots of action, you will find her sitting in front of a canvas, painting the landscape, which is so abundant around her home.

Visit her website at:
http://coffeytonya.wix.com/tonya-coffey